"Maybe you should tell them, Derek," Sharine said under her breath. "Nancy solves mysteries. She might be able to help."

You can bet *that* got my attention. "Tell us what?" I asked.

Derek stared moodily down at his feet before answering. "This isn't the first time I've been the target of this kind of trick," he began. "Up until now, it's just been notes. I got the first one about a year ago. Someone slipped it in with my gear during a race in Colorado."

"What did it say?" I asked.

Derek shrugged uncomfortably. "Something about watching my back. I didn't take it seriously," he said. With a sigh, he began putting his things back into his race bag. "I figured someone was just trying to break my concentration. But then last month I got another one."

"Derek didn't want to say anything, but I got pretty scared when he showed it to me," Sharine added. "I actually saved it. I guess I figured we might want it in case anything *else* happened."

She reached inside her own race bag, pulled out a nylon wallet, and took a crumpled piece of paper from it. She unfolded it and held it out to me.

A crude drawing of a stick figure hanging from a noose filled the top of the page. Below it, in heavy black marker, someone had written, *I'll get you when you least expect it.*

NANCY DREW
girl detective®

Available from Aladdin Paperbacks

NANCY DREW
girl detective ®

#25

Trails of Treachery

CAROLYN KEENE

Aladdin Paperbacks

New York London Toronto Sydney

❧ALADDIN PAPERBACKS
An imprint of Simon & Schuster Children's Publishing Division
1230 Avenue of the Americas, New York, NY 10020
Copyright © 2007 by Simon & Schuster, Inc.
All rights reserved, including the right of
reproduction in whole or in part in any form.
NANCY DREW, NANCY DREW: GIRL DETECTIVE, ALADDIN PAPER-
BACKS, and related logo are registered trademarks of Simon & Schuster, Inc.
Manufactured in the United States of America
First Aladdin Paperbacks edition August 2007
10 9 8 7 6 5 4
Library of Congress Control Number 2006938737
ISBN-13: 978-1-4169-3524-7
ISBN-10: 1-4169-3524-X

Contents

1

Prerace Jitters

"Can you believe we're actually here?" My friend George Fayne dropped her backpack and gazed around the sandy clearing where she stood with me and Bess Marvin. "Check it out. These bikes are amazing!"

The three of us had just walked from our hotel down a sloping path to the beach. George nodded at the shiny aluminum bicycles that dotted the ground in front of us, people bent over the frames with their tool kits at hand. Bess and I looked at each other and exchanged a grin, amused by the totally fascinated way George stared at them.

Maybe I should mention that Bess and George and I have been best friends practically since we learned to walk. When you've known one another for that long, a single glance can say a lot. I had a pretty good idea of what Bess was thinking before she even opened her mouth.

"George, we're in *Costa Rica*," she said. Bess waved a hand toward the deep-blue Pacific Ocean, which stretched out endlessly beyond the sandy cove. Sunlight sparkled off the surf, and waves broke on a perfect crescent of beach. Palm trees, orchids, and hanging vines edged the shore, and the terra cotta roofs of buildings peeked out from the trees behind us. The raucous calls of parrots echoed in the steamy afternoon air. There were even a couple of white-faced monkeys staring down at us from the branches of some nearby trees.

"We flew halfway across the continent to one of the most exotic tropical destinations in Central America—maybe even in the world," Bess went on. "And you notice the *bikes*?"

George just shrugged. "Mountain-biking is the whole reason we're here, right?" she said. "It isn't every day that I get to compete against top cyclists. Can you blame me for having bikes on the brain?"

I guess you could say George is something of a sports nut, and it definitely shows in her style. She has a closet full of shorts, T-shirts, and running shoes, and she keeps her dark hair short and simple. She might have a few dresses and skirts—but that's mostly Bess's influence. As for me, I guess I'm somewhere in the middle. I like to dress up sometimes, but I don't have the same kind of flair for fashion that Bess has. She could wear a garbage bag and still look amazing.

"The race crosses the whole country, from here to the Atlantic coast," George went on. "We'll head through rain forests, over a volcano, through coffee and banana plantations. . . . Competing in La Ruta will be a great way to see Costa Rica."

La Ruta was short for La Ruta de los Conquistadores. George had been talking about the mountain-biking race ever since she signed up for it six months ago, so I knew some of the details. In English, La Ruta de los Conquistadores means "The Route of the Conquistadors." The race retraced the same path some Spanish explorers had taken way back in the 1500s. Except that back then the Spanish had taken a couple of years to make the trip, with horses and heavy metal armor. George and the other mountain bikers had different kinds of gear—polypropylene cycling suits and titanium-alloy bikes. Not to mention that they would cover the same territory in just three days— starting bright and early the next morning.

"You've got a point. I bet we'll see parts of the country we'd never get to if you weren't in the race," Bess said, brightening. "And Nancy and I don't even have to pedal a single mile to see it all."

Bess and I had come along as George's support team. We had rented a Jeep so we could follow her progress and make sure she had first-aid supplies, spare brake pads and cables, extra clothes . . . and plenty of cheerleading. According to the race pamphlet, some parts of the trail were so remote and rough that cars and jeeps couldn't go on them. Whenever support teams like ours hit one of those spots, they would take alternate routes and meet up with the riders at checkpoints later on.

"My Spanish isn't great, but didn't the guy at the hotel desk say I should get my number and race kit here?" George asked.

She bit her lip and looked around. The beach where we stood was part of the coastal resort town of Punta Leona. We had taken a bus there after flying to the capital, San Jose. We hadn't had a chance to see much of the resort yet. But as we'd walked to the beach from our room—in one of the villas that overlooked the ocean—we'd spotted a couple of pools, an open-air restaurant with a thatched roof, and a sign for a nature preserve.

"The registration area for the race should be here somewhere," I said. Down the beach to the left I saw surfboards and sailboats. To the right, beneath a canopy of leafy trees and vines, a line of people snaked toward a tented area. A sign next to the tent read

4

Recepción. "There," I said. "That must be where you sign in."

"I hope I trained hard enough," George said, scanning the crowd as she hoisted her backpack onto her shoulder and headed toward the tent. "I've heard La Ruta can be brutal. It's got incredibly rocky trails, verticle climbs, extreme heat and humidity. . . . It's supposed to be the ultimate challenge."

I was surprised by the hint of nervousness I heard in her voice. George is usually a pretty confident person. "No one could be more ready than you are," I said truthfully. "You've gone on rides almost every day for the last six months. Not to mention all the long-distance runs, weight training, upper-body workouts. . . . You'll probably breeze through."

"Professional mountain bikers from around the world ride in La Ruta, and even some of *them* drop out," George said. She kicked up a cloud of sand with her sandal, then gave a determined smile. "But I'm going to give it my best shot. I'm not expecting to take first place or anything, but I really want to at least finish."

"That makes two of us," a voice chirped from behind us.

We turned to see a young woman with chocolate-brown skin. She wore cycling shorts and a tank top and gazed at us with sparkling amber eyes. "Hi, I'm

Sharine," she said. "My boyfriend and I flew in from San Francisco to compete. That's Derek over there."

Sharine nodded at a dark-skinned guy wearing cycling shorts and a short-sleeve shirt that showed his muscular build. He was resting his mountain bike against one of the poles that supported the reception tent.

"Derek? You mean Derek McDaniel?" George asked, peering at him with interest. "The guy who won the Rocky Mountain Challenge last month?"

"That's him." Sharine placed her nylon sports bag on the sand and began digging inside it.

"Wow," George said, letting out a whistle. She shot another glance in Derek's direction, but he was talking to someone and didn't seem to notice us. "I read about him. He's the one to beat on the mountain-biking circuit these days."

Sharine straightened up from her bag holding a water bottle; she took a long drink. "Derek's definitely on a winning streak. Some people think he's one of the top contenders to win La Ruta," she said. "I'm a decent biker, but I know Derek's going to leave me in the dust. I'm not even going to try to compete with him. Like you say, I'll be happy if I finish."

There was something so friendly and easygoing about Sharine that I couldn't help liking her. Bess, George, and I introduced ourselves.

6

"I don't know about Derek leaving you in the dust—there could be more mud than anything else," I said. "I read in my guidebook that the rainy season here doesn't end for another couple of weeks."

"Don't remind me," George said, groaning.

Sharine laughed. "Well, whether we're in dust or mud, I wouldn't mind pacing myself with another racer. Maybe we can ride together, George."

"Sure, I'd like that," George answered. She was grinning now, and the nervousness was gone from her voice. "Why don't we have dinner, too? All of us," she added, waving to include Derek, Bess, and me. "There's a prerace meeting at six, to go over rules and answer questions. We can head to dinner after that."

"Boy, you weren't kidding when you said La Ruta can be brutal, George," Bess said a few hours later. "That guy made it sound like it's tougher than climbing Mount Everest."

The prerace meeting was just breaking up. People were getting up from benches that had been set up on the sand inside the reception tent. We were all sweating—though I wasn't sure whether it was because of the steamy air or the vivid way the La Ruta official had described the race. As we filed out of the tent, I saw a lot of dazed faces, including George's.

"Rickety suspension bridges, crocodile-infested rivers, monkeys throwing coconuts from trees . . . " George murmured.

"Sounds more like a safari than a bike race," I added.

"It'll be an adventure, anyway," George said, laughing. "A race isn't worth riding if it's too easy, right?"

She smiled over her shoulder at Sharine and Derek, who were right behind us. Derek was a few years older than us—maybe in his early twenties. He was at least a head taller than Sharine, and everything about him was long and lean—his face, his arms, his incredibly muscled legs. The one soft spot he seemed to have was in his eyes. They were alert and held a shining warmth as he smiled back at us.

"You know what they say. No pain, no gain," Derek joked.

"I hope so," George said. She turned to Bess and me. "Just promise me you'll cheer me on no matter what. I don't care how tough La Ruta is. I want to be sure I get to the finish line."

"You'll do great, George," I assured her. "You've entered tons of sports competitions. There hasn't been a challenge yet that's gotten the best of you."

"Just like there hasn't been a mystery yet that's gotten the best of you," she shot back.

"Really?" Sharine asked, looking curiously at me.

"Sure," Bess answered for me. "Back home, Nancy has solved crimes even the police couldn't figure out."

I guess I *do* have a reputation for solving mysteries back in River Heights. But mysteries weren't a part of the picture at the moment.

The sun was low in the sky. It sent a shimmering, rosy glow over the darkening trees. Lanterns lit up the path we followed through the dense trees and vines, past some villas and over a footbridge to a terraced, open-air restaurant. Dozens of tables had been set up beneath a woven thatched roof. At one end was a long buffet with dishes of steaming shrimp, fried fish, grilled vegetables, and more noodle, rice, and pasta dishes than I could count. All the incredible, yummy smells made me realize how hungry I was.

"Looks like the press is here," George said under her breath. She nodded at a young man who stood near the entrance. A digital camera hid most of his face, but I saw bleached blond hair pulled back in a ponytail, a Hawaiian shirt, and a tag marked *"Prensa"* that hung from his neck by a nylon cord. I figured it had to be some kind of press pass. It banged against his shirt as he swung around to take half a dozen shots of Derek.

"Kind of makes you feel like a movie star, doesn't it?" Bess said, as the photographer moved on to someone else.

"Derek is always getting bombarded by the press since he's one of the top riders," Sharine told us. "Reporters for the big biking magazines have been trying to guess who's going to take first place."

"You're definitely one of the most favored to win, right, Derek?" George said.

Derek shrugged. "One of them, but not the only one," he said. "Ticos have the home turf advantage in this race, you know."

"Ticos?" Bess asked.

"That's what Costa Ricans call themselves," Derek explained. "Since they live here, they're used to the terrain and climate. That gives them an edge over the rest of us. See that guy with the yellow shirt?"

He nodded at a table near the buffet. Three young men sat there. One of them, a guy with dark hair, broad cheekbones, and muscular arms, wore a yellow polo shirt. They had just finished eating, and their plates were empty except for some fish bones, shrimp shells, and bits of rice. The three of them chattered in rapid-fire Spanish punctuated by laughter.

"That's Juan Santiago. He's won La Ruta for three years running," Sharine explained. "The guy's a machine. He can handle the most extreme conditions—mud, heat, the steepest, rockiest hills. Nothing stops him."

We passed the Costa Ricans as we headed toward

the buffet. Derek paused at their table, and all three guys stopped talking.

"Hi, there. *Hola*," Derek said. "We're going to be seeing a lot of each other over the next three days, so I figured I'd introduce myself. I'm—"

"I know who you are," Juan interrupted, in lightly accented English. I noticed he didn't return Derek's smile.

"I, uh, just wanted to wish you luck in the race," Derek went on. He held out his hand. "May the best man win."

I saw a camera flash out of the corner of my eye. Neither Derek nor Juan paid any attention to it. Juan made no move to shake Derek's hand. Pushing back his chair, he got up and said, "You'll need a lot more than luck to win La Ruta."

He and his friends walked off, leaving Derek's hand hanging.

2

Face-Off

For a moment, Derek just stood there with his mouth wide open.

"What's his problem?" Bess muttered under her breath.

I was wondering the same thing. We were all kind of dazed as we moved toward the buffet—until a blinding flash of light stopped us in our tracks. The photographer with the blond ponytail had leaped in front of us with his camera.

"Beautiful," he murmured, taking shot after shot of Derek's scowling face. "I can see the headline now. 'Champion and Challenger Face Off at La Ruta.'"

I wasn't crazy about the guy's in-your-face style, but Derek managed to ignore him. He kept his eyes on Juan, who had stopped to play soccer with a bunch of kids outside the restaurant. It was only when Juan and the kids kicked the ball out of sight that Derek finally turned to look at the photographer.

"Gee, I'm glad you're so happy about my first run-in with the competition," he said sarcastically. "Still photographing for *Off-Road*, Paul?"

"*Off-Road Adventures*? I love that magazine!" George spoke up. Turning to Bess and me, she explained, "You should have seen the spread they did on a bike trek through the Australian outback last year. The photos made you feel like you were right there."

The photographer smiled and gave a little bow. "It's nice to know people appreciate my work," he said. "And yes, I'll be covering La Ruta . . . especially the competition between the top riders." He lowered his camera and fixed Derek with a probing look. "Think you can get ahead of Juan Santiago?"

"Sure, why not? That's what I've been training for," Derek told him.

"If anyone can get past Juan, it's Derek. You've seen him race enough to know that, Paul," Sharine added. "By the way, Nancy, Bess, and George, meet Paul Maynard. He happens to be one of the best sports photographers around, so Derek puts up with his pestering us endlessly with that camera of his. Paul has covered almost every race Derek's ridden in."

"Sounds like exciting work," Bess said.

"It'll do," Paul told her. "What can I say? Taking photos of mountain biking is the next best thing to actually competing. I had to quit racing after I hurt my back in an accident a few years back. But taking photos keeps me close to the thrill of it. Almost makes me feel like I'm in the middle of the pack on my bike."

"Well, I hope you get a few shots of George while you're covering the race," Bess said, nodding at Paul's high-tech silver camera. "They'll probably come out a lot better than the pictures Nancy and I will take with my old point-and-shoot."

"Actually, you can take some pretty impressive photos with a point-and-shoot," he said, flashing her a wide smile. "If you want, I'll show you some of the tricks of the trade to help you get better pictures of George. We're going to be seeing some incredible biking."

The way Paul talked, it was obvious he really loved the sport. I was starting to warm up to the guy. And he was definitely warming up to Bess. As we grabbed plates and made our way down the buffet, he seemed to forget he was supposed to be taking pictures. He stuck close to Bess's side—bending her ear about camera angles and action shots—while we loaded our plates with grilled fish, shrimp, ribs, some kind of fried greens, and an amazing-looking mango salad.

I was just reaching for some bread when an elbow jabbed into my ribs and nearly made me drop my plate.

"Huh?" I recovered my balance and frowned at the petite, birdlike woman who'd pushed past me. She had blond hair that was cut bluntly just below her ears. Her tailored pants suit and crisp linen blouse stood out among all the casual athletic clothes and sun visors. She stepped purposefully over to Derek and grabbed his arm.

"There you are, Derek! I've been looking everywhere for you," she said.

The woman didn't seem to notice that the rest of us were there. She steered Derek away from the buffet without a word to anyone else. "I've just had a telephone conference with Aqua Trim. . . . "

"Did we suddenly become invisible?" George murmured, frowning. "Who *is* that?"

"Cynthia Goldman. She's Derek's agent," Sharine explained.

"Derek has an agent?" I said. I guess I shouldn't have been so surprised. Everyone knows there's big money in competitive sports. Companies spend millions to have sports stars advertise their products.

"Sure," Sharine answered. "Cynthia's in the middle of negotiating a deal with Aqua Trim."

"The sports-drink company?" George said.

15

Sharine nodded. "They want Derek to use their products when he races, maybe do some commercials."

Cynthia and Derek were already sitting down at one of the tables. When we joined them, Cynthia turned to Paul with a bright smile. "I'm counting on you to make sure Derek's photo is plastered all over the next issues of *Off-Road*," she said.

"Hey, I just take the pictures," Paul said, holding up his hands. "It's up to Derek to win the race."

"Oh, he will," Cynthia said confidently. "But Derek's challenge to the top Costa Rican riders is big news, whether or not he wins. Talk to the other journalists. Make sure Derek gets the attention he deserves. That's all I'm asking. Publicity is everything, after all."

I wasn't sure I agreed with her. And I could tell that George didn't. She scowled at Cynthia as we sat down at the table. "What ever happened to just going out and doing your best to win?" she said. "I thought *that* was the whole point of races like La Ruta."

Cynthia blinked, as if she had just now realized we were there. Even after Derek introduced us, the agent's expression was cool. "Biking for the personal challenge is a lovely idea, of course," she said, in a voice that held no enthusiasm. "But professional sports is a little more complicated."

"I compete because I love it," Derek insisted. "I've

always loved mountain biking. But a little publicity can't hurt. The more publicity I get during this race . . ."

"The better the deal Cynthia will be able to make with Aqua Trim?" I guessed.

Cynthia turned to me with a smug smile. "I see you get the picture after all," she said.

I guess she had a point. But for the rest of dinner we had to listen to her drone on about press conferences and photo shoots and her negotiations with Aqua Trim. Much as I liked Derek and Sharine, I was relieved when Bess, George, and I said good night and headed back to our villa. After all, the race was going to start at five o'clock the next morning. We needed to focus on George, not some endorsement deal. And that meant early to bed, and early to rise.

We were all pretty excited—and nervous. But eventually we drifted off to sleep with a chorus of chirps, howls, and songs echoing in the humid darkness outside our windows.

Beep! Beep! Beep!

George's digital alarm woke me way too early the next morning. I cracked open an eye, then groaned into our pitch-black room.

"Three thirty . . . in the morning?" I croaked out, staring at the glowing numbers of the clock on the dresser.

"Can't we just sleep for another fifteen minutes?" Bess's muffled voice came from beneath her pillow.

"No way," George said. The lamp next to her clicked on, and I saw that she was already sitting up in bed. She swung her feet to the floor and reached for the biking shorts she'd laid out the night before. "The race starts in an hour and a half. How can you even think of sleeping?"

Bess and I managed to rouse ourselves, but George was definitely moving in a faster gear. She was practically dressed before Bess and I even got out of bed. While we put on our shorts and T-shirts, George checked, double-checked, and then triple-checked her sports bag and tool kit.

"Water bottle, wrenches, cable cutters, extra brake pads, spare T-shirt, sunscreen . . . ," she murmured. George pinned her number—228—to the front of her T-shirt. Grabbing her yellow helmet, she took one last look in her bag and zipped it up. "I'm all set. We just have to pick up my bike from the security truck and grab a bite from the breakfast buffet."

The race organizers had really thought of everything. Mechanics were traveling along the race route and could be hired to tune up bikes for anyone who wanted. George had made arrangements with a mechanic named Miguel to take care of her bike. Bikes were stored in securely locked trucks overnight, so Miguel had told her to pick her bike up there before the race.

As we made our way to the trucks, in the parking lot outside the resort's main building, I could already feel the humidity building. Sweat beaded on my forehead, but George was so nervous and excited that she didn't seem to notice the heat. After she got her bike she checked it over quickly and wheeled it toward the main building.

The big reception area was already crowded when we got there. As we pulled open the door, George glanced around. It was a madhouse, with bikes, bikers, and gear bags all over. Couches, chairs, and potted plants dotted the reception area, but the place still looked more like a bike shop than a hotel. Bikers filled every seat and mobbed the registration area and buffet table. It took us a few minutes to get through the crowd so we could grab some Danish and papaya. I guess we were all pretty nervous, because we ate in about ten seconds flat.

"I want to wish Sharine and Derek good luck before we head to the starting line," George said, as she wheeled her bike away from the buffet. "Hmm . . . Over there."

She pointed toward an alcove near the front desk. Sharine and Derek were sitting together. They both wore cycling shorts and shirts. Derek's blue race bag was open on the floor in front of him. He bent over it, hurriedly yanking things out and tossing them aside. Derek's calm confidence had disappeared. His eyes had a panicked gleam.

"What's the matter?" George asked, stopping her bike next to them.

Derek barely glanced at her. "It's gone," he murmured. He dumped out some brake cables and a shirt, and then looked in his bag again. "I know I packed it, but now it's not here. . . . "

"*What's* not here?" I asked.

"Derek's tool kit," Sharine answered. "It's missing."

"I never ride without my tool kit. I packed it myself this morning. If it's missing, there's only one possible explanation," Derek insisted.

He sat back on his heels and blew out a frustrated breath. "Somebody must have stolen it."

3

Thief at La Ruta

S tolen? Are you sure?" I asked. I gazed down at the pile of clothes and supplies that Derek had dumped from his bag. "You couldn't have misplaced it?"

Even as I made the suggestion, I knew how ridiculous it sounded. A professional like Derek must have ridden in hundreds of races. He wouldn't misplace something as important as his tools.

"Someone stole it," he said again. "Someone who wants to make sure I don't win La Ruta."

The fear in his eyes hardened to anger, but I noticed that Sharine kept fidgeting. She looked more and more anxious. "Maybe you should tell them, Derek," she said under her breath. "Nancy solves mysteries. She might be able to help."

You can bet *that* got my attention. "Tell us what?" I asked.

Derek stared moodily down at his feet before answering. "This isn't the first time I've been the target of this kind of trick," he began.

"What do you mean?" George asked. She sat on the arm of Sharine's chair while Bess and I dropped down to sit on the floor.

"Up until now, it's just been notes," Derek explained. "I got the first one about a year ago. Someone slipped it in with my gear during a race in Colorado."

"What did it say?" I asked.

Derek shrugged uncomfortably. "Something about watching my back. I didn't take it seriously," he said. With a sigh, he began putting his things back into his race bag. "I figured someone was just trying to break my concentration. But then last month I got another one."

"Derek didn't want to say anything, but I got pretty scared when he showed it to me," Sharine added. "I actually saved it. I guess I figured we might want it in case anything *else* happened."

She reached inside her own race bag, pulled out a nylon wallet, and took a crumpled piece of paper from it. She unfolded it and held it out to me.

A crude drawing of a stick figure hanging from a noose filled the top of the page. Below it, in heavy black marker, someone had written, *I'll get you when you least expect it.*

"No wonder you were worried," Bess said, grimacing. "You think whoever wrote that took Derek's tool kit?"

"Um, guys?" George spoke up, before Sharine could answer. She glanced toward the hotel entrance, nervously fidgeting with the strap of her helmet. "Riders are starting to head out to the starting line. I know this is a big deal, and we've got to do something. But . . ."

"The only thing *you* need to do is get to the starting line," Sharine said firmly. "Save me a place, okay? I'll catch up with you as soon as I can."

"I'll go with you, George," Bess said. She dug in her bag for the keys to our rented Jeep. "Nancy, are you coming?"

I must have hesitated. Not that I didn't want to go with George. I was her support team—or half of it, anyway. But when a mystery grabs me, I get totally caught up in it. All kinds of questions had popped into my mind. I couldn't just ignore them.

"Give me ten minutes," I said, glancing at my watch. "We've still got over half an hour before the race begins. I'll find you at the starting line."

George was already heading toward the entrance with her bike. She wasn't the only one. A river of cyclists flowed out the door. I had to move fast before the place emptied out completely.

"Did you come straight here after you left your room?" I asked, turning to Derek. "Did you stop anywhere? Or notice anyone near your race bag?"

Derek had finished putting his things in his pack. "I picked up my bike at the security truck," he said. "After that I came straight here to meet Sharine. We haven't moved our bikes since we got here, and we've been sitting right here. . . . "

"Except when we got that phone call," Sharine put in.

Derek blinked—then slapped the palm of his hand against his forehead. "That's right! The guy at the front desk paged us. Said we had a phone call."

"Both of you?" I asked.

"Yeah. We figured it was someone from home calling to wish us luck. But when we went to the phone, no one was on the line," he said. He nodded toward a phone that sat on one end of the hotel desk.

"Whoever took your tools must have had you paged as a distraction," I guessed. "While you went to the phone, he took your tools. The question is . . . "

"Who did it?" Sharine finished. Frowning, she glanced around at all the bikers, race officials, journalists, and support crews. "I didn't notice anyone near our stuff. But there are people all over the place—it's not exactly easy to keep track."

That was the understatement of the year. Still, I wasn't about to give up. "Well, if those notes came from the same person, it must be someone who's competed in some of the same races as you," I said, thinking out loud.

"There must be twenty or thirty people here that I've raced with in the past year. Maybe more," Derek said. Straightening away from his bike, he slung his race bag over his shoulder. "Anyway, I can't worry about it now. I've got to get some new tools before the race starts."

He headed toward some race officials who stood near the registration table. Sharine reached for her own bike, then paused to look at me. "Do you think you can help?" she asked. "I mean, what if the person who took Derek's tools tries something else? La Ruta is hard enough without worrying that someone is out to get him."

"I'll take a look around and see what I can find out," I promised. "Is there anything distinctive about Derek's tool kit?"

Sharine thought for a moment. "The pliers and wrenches and cable cutters have yellow rubber handles, but most of the tools are just metal," she said. "They were in a black nylon case . . . nothing special."

Hmm. That didn't make my job any easier. And

more people were heading out to the starting line, which meant that suspects could be leaving too. The only good thing was that it was easier to look around without so many bikes and people clogging the place. I walked slowly from one end of the reception area to the other, looking under chairs and in corners. There were half a dozen alcoves like the one where we'd been sitting with Derek and Sharine. The first two were empty. But in the third, I hit the jackpot. Two pairs of pliers lay behind a leafy potted fern. They had bright yellow rubber handles.

"Bingo!" I murmured, picking them up.

I looked quickly around—and did a double take when I saw who was sitting just half a dozen feet away.

"Juan?" I said.

I recognized Juan Santiago's broad face from the restaurant the night before. Today he wore a red cycling shirt and black shorts. He and the two riders he'd had dinner with were just getting up from their chairs. Juan turned distractedly toward me as he reached for his bike.

"Yes?" he said.

"I just found these on the floor over there," I said, holding up the pliers. "I'm pretty sure they belong to Derek McDaniel."

Juan frowned slightly. "So?" he said.

"Someone took his tool kit from his bag this

morning. Did you know that?" I pressed.

Juan took his time tugging on a pair of biking gloves. He said something to his friends in Spanish, and they laughed. But when he spoke to me, his face and expression were totally neutral.

"I'm sorry to hear it," he said. "Please excuse me. The race will start soon."

Talk about frustrating! All I could do was watch while Juan and his friends wheeled their bikes away. Checking my watch, I saw that it was after four thirty. My ten minutes were definitely up. I hurried from the main building.

The sun hadn't yet begun to rise. The warm, humid night air was like a black velvet veil that hung over everything. A path snaked through the trees. Lanterns along it sent a hazy glow over the crowd of people and bikes that swarmed toward the main road of Punta Leona. As I got closer, I saw that the pack of racers stretched back a couple hundred yards from the starting line. Spectators stood three and four deep along the sides of the road. I squeezed through the crowd, scanning the anxious faces of the riders.

"Nancy!" I heard Bess's voice, then saw her waving from the edge of the road about twenty feet away. George and Sharine were in front of her, on their bikes and ready to go.

I waved back, holding up the pliers I'd found. "Be

there in a second!" I shouted. "I have to find . . . "

"Me?" a man's voice spoke up behind me.

I turned to see Derek wheeling his bike along the path toward me. His gloves and neon-green helmet were on, and the number 139 was pinned to his jersey and to the handlebars of his bike. His face lit up when he saw the pliers in my hand.

"Great! You found my tools?" he said, taking them.

"Then, they *are* yours?" I asked.

Derek nodded. He listened while I told him about finding the tools and talking to Juan. But his attention was definitely on the race, not on me. We kept getting jostled to the side by other riders on their way to the starting line. Derek's eyes flitted over the crowd, and he kept inching his bike closer to the pack.

"Well, whoever took my tools isn't going to slow me down this time," he said, when I was finished. "I went to Miguel—he's the guy who tuned up my bike yesterday."

"One of the mechanics?" I asked. "I think he tuned up George's bike too."

"Well, luckily for me, he had an extra set of tools, and now I've got them." Derek patted his race bag, then wheeled his bike past me. "Wish me luck!"

"Good luck!" I told him. Actually, I kind of

shouted it at his back, since he was already in the thick crowd.

I made my way back to where Bess, George, and Sharine stood as quickly as possible. The sky had gone from black to gray, and there was a yellow radiance above the mountains to the east where the sun would soon rise. In the pale light, I could see the tense excitement on George's face. She and Sharine were happy to hear that Derek had gotten new tools. Not that we had much time to talk.

"We'd better get to our Jeep, Nancy," said Bess. She nodded at the line of cars and ATVs that snaked along the far side of the road. "It looks like a lot of the other support teams are already in place. The race is going to start in less than ten minutes!"

It seemed like everyone in Costa Rica had come to Punta Leona to see the start of the race. People were jammed in everywhere. Luckily, La Ruta officials kept a narrow lane clear for support crews. Bess and I reached the back of the line of cars just in time to hear the *bang!* of the starter's pistol.

"They're off!" Bess cried, amid the deafening cheers of the crowd. She stood up in the Jeep, holding up her camera as the dense mob of bikers began to move past us. "They're all so close!" she said. "How do they keep from knocking into one another?"

I wondered the same thing. It seemed like there was barely any space between the riders, and they were starting to pick up speed.

"There's Derek," I said, pointing at his neon-green helmet. I was glad to see he was near the front of the pack, but within seconds my view of him was blocked by the wall of bikers coming up behind. The support vehicles weren't moving yet, so Bess and I just sat and watched, keeping on the alert for George's yellow helmet.

"There she is!" Bess squealed, after a few minutes.

A thrill shot through me when I spotted a splash of yellow among the riders, and then George's determined face. Bess snapped a picture, and we both started cheering like crazy. George glanced at us and grinned, giving us the thumbs-up sign.

In that exact second, two bikers in front of her caught their wheels together. I gasped as the bikes went down with a crash.

"Look out!" Bess shouted.

More riders rammed into them, unable to avoid the fallen bikes. I don't know how George managed it, but she turned sharply, just missing the pile.

"Yes!" I crowed, as she pedaled smoothly ahead.

The race was on.

4

Off-Road Intrigue

How far until the first checkpoint?" I asked Bess.

I squinted into the sunlight, which pounded down on our Jeep. The sun had been up for less than an hour, but already the temperature was up over ninety degrees. The jungle air felt so humid that I was sure we could squeeze water from it if we tried hard enough. Bess and I had on baseball hats and sunglasses, but we were still sweating. If we were this hot just sitting in our Jeep, I couldn't imagine how George must feel.

"The race info says the first checkpoint is at twenty-eight kilometers, and we've already gone about twelve," Bess said, glancing at the odometer on our dashboard.

I did the math in my head. The total distance

for the first day—which the organizers called Stage One—was about 115 kilometers. "So George and Sharine are only about one tenth of the way through Stage One," I realized. "Not to mention that most of it has been straight up."

The first few miles of the race had followed the coastline. But then the route had turned onto a muddy road that rose up sharply. Riders had begun slipping and sweating, and even a few of the support ATVs had trouble negotiating the climb.

Bess and I were keeping pace with George and Sharine in our Jeep. From what I could tell, they were doing pretty well. I had only seen one woman ahead of them so far. But their faces were serious, and their jerseys were soaked with sweat. They barely seemed to notice the spectacular views of the Pacific Ocean that appeared whenever there was a break in the trees.

"Hmm." I frowned when I saw a biker who was kneeling over his bike in the mud, fixing a flat tire. "No wonder Derek was so upset about his tools being taken," I said. "That's the third person we've seen making repairs."

Up ahead, the muddy road curved into the jungle once more. I was glad for the shade, especially when I caught sight of a gorgeous, brightly colored parrot with a long red tail and splashes of blue and yellow on its wings.

"A scarlet macaw!" I said, pointing to the leafy branches where the bird was perched.

"Wow," Bess said, angling a look at it. "Our guidebook says there are over a dozen other kinds of parrots too. Actually, there are more kinds of birds in Costa Rica than in all of North America."

She aimed her camera and pressed the shutter—then frowned. "Rats. The battery's dead," she said. "And I didn't bring any extras."

"Maybe we can get one of those disposable cameras when we stop," I suggested.

I hit the brake as the battered pickup truck ahead of me slowed down. It looked as if George and Sharine and the other bikers were slowing down too. Peering ahead up the road, I saw why. A yellow La Ruta marker directed racers off the road and onto an even smaller trail.

Following the lead of the racers in front of them, George and Sharine got off their bikes. I wasn't sure why, until I caught sight of the new part of the course. It didn't look like a trail as much as a wall of rocky mud. Hoisting their bikes up onto their shoulders, George and Sharine began hiking up the steep, slippery path on foot.

"Looks like the race route gets pretty technical here," I said.

"There's no way anyone could ride a bike up that,"

Bess commented, shaking her head in disbelief.

"Or drive," I added. "This must be one of the places where the support crews branch off from the racers."

Sure enough, all the ATVs, cars, and trucks continued along the main road. I beeped our horn, and Bess called out the window, "Meet you at the checkpoint!" Then we drove around a bend, and George and Sharine were out of sight.

It took us another hour to get to the first checkpoint—a stopping place where bikers could get drinks and snacks. The road leading there went through some pretty remote rain forest. We kept slowing down to look at monkeys, sloths, parrots, and incredibly colorful butterflies. As amazing as the scenery was, I was glad when we reached the checkpoint, in a little village that consisted of some small houses and a snack bar clustered by the road.

It looked like the kind of place that was sleepy most of the time. Not today. The organizers of La Ruta had parked a service truck nearby where racers could get sports drinks and snacks. Next to it was a first-aid tent that was marked with a red cross. People swarmed around both areas and filled the snack bar—a tin-roofed building made of cinder blocks that had been painted turquoise. People sat at half a dozen tables outside, drinking sodas and eating tacos or chips. Through the open doorway, I saw more people sitting inside. Still, as Bess and I parked off the side of the road, I found myself seeking out racers, not spectators.

"No bikers. At least, not yet," I said, shading my eyes from the sun.

"No, but there's Paul Maynard." Bess pointed toward the snack bar. Paul was sitting at one of the tables outside, wearing a different Hawaiian shirt from the one he'd had on the day before. For once, he wasn't taking pictures. His camera case sat on the table in front of him, next to a bottle of soda and a plate of something. His face lit up when he saw Bess.

"Hi, there! Why don't you join me?" he called.

I shot a teasing grin at Bess as she waved back. "Is it my imagination, or has Paul been flirting with you since we met him?" I whispered.

"He means for *both* of us to hang out with him," Bess said, rolling her eyes. "Anyway, it's not like we're going to start going out or something. He just seems like a nice guy, that's all."

When we got to his table, Paul smiled and held up his glass. "I figured I might as well get a cool drink while I wait for the first riders. These little soda joints usually have great food. My fried tortillas are fantastic."

A few minutes later, Bess and I were sipping lime sodas and munching on some tortilla sandwiches.

Paul had been following the front riders, and he told us all about the photos he'd taken at the start of the race. Actually, he mostly talked with Bess while I kept my eye on the road. I kept picturing the note Sharine had shown us. After what had happened this morning, I was pretty nervous for Derek. I really hoped he was all right.

"According to this, there are four checkpoints," Bess said, scanning through a La Ruta pamphlet that she'd pulled from her bag. "Bikers have to get to each one by a certain time, or they're disqualified," she said.

"That's right, the cutoff for this checkpoint is almost two hours away," Paul said. "But the top racers will come through long before that. The last I saw, Derek and Juan were still fighting it out for first. They kept leapfrogging in front of each other."

He gulped down the last of his soda, then grinned at us. Reaching for his camera, he stood up. "Back in my racing days, you would have seen *me* at the head of the pack," he said. There was a slight wistfulness in his voice, but then he shook himself. "Today, Derek's the one to watch. When he gets here, I'll be ready."

"It figures that my camera would run out of batteries," Bess said, rolling her eyes. She pointed toward the snack shop. "Do you think they sell disposable cameras here?"

"Forget that," Paul told her. "I always bring a lot

more equipment than I need. I have three other digital cameras locked in my car. One of them would be perfect for you. It's good, but not so expensive that you have to worry about it."

"Really? You wouldn't mind?" Bess said.

Paul shot her a wide smile. "Definitely not," he said. He strode over to a mud-splattered green car and came back with a camera that was about half the size of the one he was using.

"It's a pretty basic model," he said. "You can put it on automatic, but if you want to play with the settings . . ."

I was too distracted to listen to his instructions. I kept glancing down the road to where the racers would appear. A few yellow flags marked the route. I could only see the final hundred yards or so where the trail emerged from a dense stand of trees and then sloped down a rocky hillside to the road where the checkpoint was.

Reaching into my bag, I pulled out a pair of binoculars I had brought. I trained them on the yellow marker that showed where the race route came out of the trees. More and more people were showing up in their ATVs—reporters and people like Bess and me who were there to support the racers. I spotted Cynthia Goldman hovering near the La Ruta truck. It looked like she was chatting up a couple of guys wearing press passes, but I didn't look closely. Mostly, I kept my binoculars trained on that yellow marker near the trees.

"Anything yet?" Paul asked me.

"Just a bunch of trees and—" I gasped as I caught a flash of neon green among the branches. "Wait! I think that's . . . " I jumped to my feet, keeping my binoculars trained on the green. "Yes!" I said, as I spotted the number 139 on the front of the rider's jersey. "It's Derek . . . and he's in the lead!"

All around us people started cheering like crazy. I wasn't sure Derek could hear them, but he was really moving fast. His bike hurtled down the rocky hillside, faster and faster. I heard the rapid-fire *click-click-click-click* of Paul's camera next to me.

"Fantastic!" he murmured. But there was something about the way Derek rode that bothered me.

"He's going so fast!" Bess exclaimed.

I was too busy holding my breath to respond. Derek was moving so swiftly that his wheels started bouncing and jerking unsteadily. Even with my binoculars, I couldn't get a clear view of his face. But a feeling in my gut told me something was very wrong.

All of a sudden, his bike swerved sharply, kicking up mud and rocks. A gasp went up from the crowd. I don't know how, but Derek managed to keep his balance. His bike kept hurtling wildly over the uneven ground.

"He's out of control!" I said.

"Oh my gosh," Bess breathed. "He'd better watch out for that—

Bam!

Derek's front wheel dropped into a sudden dip in the hillside. It stopped him cold, making his whole bike flip over. All I could do was stare in horror as Derek flew head over heels.

He hit the ground hard, and lay there without moving.

5

Sabotage

"He needs help!" I shouted.

Cries of alarm rang into the air. Out of the corner of my eye, I saw people rushing from the first-aid area. Not that I stuck around to see what they were doing. I was already running up the road toward Derek, my binoculars banging against my ribs.

Up on the hillside, Derek still hadn't budged. "*Please* be okay," I muttered under my breath.

It took a while, but as I scrambled up the hillside toward him, Derek finally moved. He lifted his head, then rolled onto his side and struggled to sit up.

Cheers rose from the crowd at the checkpoint. I figured they were for Derek, but then I saw that *another* biker had emerged from the trees. I recognized Juan Santiago's close-fitting red shirt. His bike bounced over the uneven terrain. His face was a blur as he rode past Derek down toward the checkpoint.

Paul and some other photographers were snapping photos like crazy from the road just below. A big shout went up as Juan reached the checkpoint, but I didn't keep watching. Turning back to Derek, I dropped down next to him.

"Are you all right?" I asked.

"I . . . think so." Derek tentatively moved his arms and legs. As he stood up, I saw a cut on his shin and scratches on his arms and legs. His chest heaved as he tried to catch his breath, but he didn't seem to have any serious injuries. Two guys with a stretcher and a first-aid kit came running up to us, but Derek waved them off.

"I'm fine," he insisted. Still, I wasn't sure that was a hundred percent true. There was a haunted look in his eyes, and his voice was shaky when he spoke.

"My brake cable . . . It snapped, just like that. I couldn't believe it!" he said. "I mean, Miguel tuned it up from top to bottom yesterday. It should be in perfect condition."

"Miguel? The mechanic?" I asked.

Derek nodded. Scowling, he walked over to his bike, which still lay half in the ditch that had made him flip over. The front tire was flat, and the frame was scratched and splattered with mud. At least it didn't look bent or broken. Another rider cycled past us, his tires kicking up mud, but Derek ignored him.

"There! Look at the cable." He fingered the metal cable that ran along the bike frame from the handlebars to the brake pads. The cable had snapped in two, and the frayed ends stuck out. It was only when I looked closely that I realized that only one side of each snapped end was frayed. The other side had been smoothly sliced.

"Someone cut partway through the cable," I said. "Your brakes worked for a while, but the cable snapped under the pressure of this rocky downhill ride."

"Which is exactly what the person wanted, I bet," Derek muttered.

"Did you check your bike over after Miguel worked on it?" I asked.

Derek shook his head. "I was going to, but instead I had to run around looking for new tools," he muttered. His scowl deepened as yet another biker rode past us, his La Ruta number flapping against the handlebars. "And now I've got a flat *and* I've lost the lead. I don't have time for this—I've got to get back in the race."

He picked up his bike and began wheeling it toward the checkpoint at a jog. Half a dozen cameras were pointed at him. La Ruta officials were keeping everyone back, but I noticed that Derek's agent managed to squeeze past. Cynthia hurried toward us, her pumps slipping on the muddy hillside.

"Can you still ride? You're not out of the race, are you?" she asked worriedly.

I couldn't help rolling my eyes. Obviously, winning was higher on Cynthia's priority list than Derek's safety. I would have expected her to show a little concern when he told her about the sliced cable. Instead, she acted like she'd just won the lottery.

"Sabotage? Oh, the press is going to have a field day with this!" she said, chortling. "You'll be all over tonight's news." Her gaze flickered toward the press. "Just get back in the race. If you can finish the day in the top three, you've still got a shot to win."

Derek seemed relieved when Cynthia moved on to the reporters. More riders were appearing, but Derek ignored everyone while he grabbed a sports drink, opened his tool kit, and went to work on his bike.

"Nancy! Is Derek all right?" Bess asked, coming over from the snack bar.

"For now. Where's Juan?" I said. Shading my eyes, I glanced toward the service truck where bikers were wolfing down sandwiches and sports drinks. Juan was just tossing aside an empty bottle with some neon-yellow dregs at the bottom of it. Getting on his bike, he adjusted his helmet and gloves.

"Juan! Can I talk to you for a second?" I called.

But he was already pedaling down the road away from us. If he heard me, he didn't stop.

"I know that look," Bess spoke up from behind me. I turned to see her gazing probingly at me with her hands on her hips. "Something is up. What is it, Nancy?"

She was pretty shocked when I told her about Derek's brake cable. "You think Juan did it?" she asked.

"He *was* near where I found Derek's missing pliers back at Punta Leona," I said. "But that's not enough to prove that he took them *or* that he sliced the brake cable."

"I just hope the accident doesn't slow Derek down too much," Bess said, as we made our way beyond the La Ruta service truck to where Derek was working on his bike. He had already replaced the brake cable and was banging on the rim of his front tire where it had bent a little.

"I guess whoever sent me those notes was serious, huh?" he said. I noticed the tight set of his jaw as he took a new tube, placed it around the rim, and used a hand-held pump to inflate it. "This is only the first day," he went on. "Who knows what the guy will try next?"

"It's not fair. You deserve to ride a clean race," Bess said.

"We'll do everything we can to find out who sliced the cable," I promised. "And stop them from doing anything else."

Derek flashed me a grateful smile. But when he rode off a few minutes later, I couldn't help wondering *how* Bess and I would find the culprit. As we stood there in the heat, with more racers starting to arrive, I tried to piece together what we knew so far.

"Derek told me his bike was in perfect condition when Miguel finished working on it yesterday," I said.

"Miguel?" Bess repeated. "You mean George's mechanic?"

I nodded. "Derek hired him too. Miguel was the last person to work on the bike," I explained.

"We should definitely talk to him," Bess said.

Not that it was easy to find the guy. People were all over the place now. Racers were arriving by the dozens, sweaty and red-faced. The checkpoint was a madhouse of bikers, reporters, photographers, support crews, and locals who'd come to cheer on the racers. Bess and I saw plenty of people making adjustments to bikes. Some of them might have been mechanics who knew Miguel, but everyone was working so fast and hard that they didn't have time for our questions. We had to give up after three people waved us away.

"Looks like we'll have to wait until after the racers finish for the day," I said.

"Maybe we should get some pointers from Cynthia Goldman. She doesn't seem to be having any trouble getting people's attention," Bess put in. "Well, the press's attention, anyway."

She nodded toward a circle of journalists who were clustered around Cynthia outside the snack bar. "It was *sabotage*," I heard her say. "Someone is out to get Derek. But it'll take a lot more than this to put him out of the running to win." She paused to look each reporter in the eye. "Derek is a professional. I have every confidence that he'll regain the lead before the end of the day. . . . "

I rolled my eyes as Bess and I circled around the reporters and sat back down at the table where we'd left our sodas and the last bits of our tortilla sandwiches. "Cynthia may be good at making sure Derek is front-page news," I said under my breath. "But I doubt it's going to help us find whoever sabotaged his bike."

Monkeys chattered from the trees on either side of the road, their screeches mixing with the cheers of the crowd. As we waited for George—and waited—I tuned out the noise and thought. So far, Derek's tool kit had been taken and his brake cable had been sabotaged. It made sense that a competitor was behind the attacks. And out of all the other riders in La Ruta, Juan was the one who was most threatened by Derek. If only I could find out whether he'd been in the two races back in the States where Derek had gotten those threatening notes . . .

"Where *is* she?" Bess said, breaking into my thoughts.

By now, Paul and most of the other photographers and reporters had moved on toward the next checkpoint. We still hadn't seen any sign of George—or Sharine. I'm not sure how long we sat there—long enough to see dozens of muddy bikers reach the checkpoint. Some were so winded they could hardly move. Others were dehydrated and had to be carried to the first-aid tent on stretchers. Bess and I waited at the snack bar, getting more and more worried.

Finally, just fifteen minutes before the cutoff, she cruised in. Except that maybe *cruising* wasn't the best way to describe it. George was drenched in sweat. Her teeth were clenched, and her face was tight and tired. Mud was splattered all over her clothes, bike, and helmet. As she came to a stop next to the refreshment truck, her breath came in ragged gasps.

"George!" Bess cried, as we ran over.

George got off her bike and bent over with her hands on her knees. She had to catch her breath for a minute before she could take the sports drink that Bess held out to her.

"This heat . . . It's . . . brutal," she said, after gulping down half the bottle. "We had a couple of monster climbs. And the downhill sections weren't much better." She looked at us, still breathing hard. "What if I don't finish the rest of the course before the cutoff time?"

For a second, Bess and I just stared at each other.

George was the ultimate competitor, and she was in great shape. If La Ruta was too hard for her, should we really push her to finish?

"Just do the best you can," Bess said. "I mean, it doesn't really matter if you finish after the official cutoff time, does it?"

"It matters to me," George insisted. "I don't want to be disqualified—not on the very first day."

She barely managed a tired smile when Sharine rode up beside us, looking just as hot and exhausted as George. Straddling her bike, Sharine reached for a sports drink and downed the whole thing in about fifteen seconds. She wiped her mouth with the back of her hand and gave a weak smile. "Well, we made it before the cutoff. Just three more checkpoints to go before we finish Stage One, George," she said.

She got off her bike and grabbed a peanut-butter-and-jelly sandwich from the truck. She wolfed down a few bites, then looked at Bess and me. "Did you see Derek?" she asked.

I wasn't sure how much to tell her. I didn't want worries about Derek to make the day even harder for Sharine and George. But Sharine must have seen the way Bess and I looked at each other.

"What? What happened?" she pressed. Bess and I filled her in. As she listened, her expression grew more and more serious.

"He's not hurt," Bess reassured her, after giving her the details. "Cynthia thinks he can make up the time before the end of the day."

"And Bess and I are doing our best to figure out who cut the cable," I added. "I want to talk to Juan, and the mechanic who worked on his bike. . . ."

"That's great. Really fantastic," George put in.

It took me a second to realize she was being sarcastic. "What's the matter?" Bess asked.

"Nothing." George swallowed the rest of her sandwich, then reached for her bike. "It's just that . . . Oh, never mind."

"What?" I said.

George didn't answer right away. All of a sudden she seemed totally focused on readjusting her bicycle seat.

"George! Talk to us," Bess said, waving a hand in front of her face.

George got on her bike, frowning the whole time. "Look, it's great that you're helping Derek. But I can't worry about him right now, okay? I've got to think about my own race—which isn't going so great, in case you hadn't noticed."

She snapped on the safety strap of her helmet and mumbled, "See you at the next checkpoint . . . if I make it that far."

Then she was gone.

6

Unanswered Questions

"Ouch," I said, as I watched George disappear into the dense jungle. "I guess I *can* be kind of single-minded when I'm working on a case. But the last thing I want is to make George feel bad."

"I guess it's partly my fault," Sharine put in. "I asked you to help Derek."

"George is usually totally on board when Nancy investigates," Bess said.

"La Ruta is a lot tougher than either of us thought it would be," Sharine said. "Some riders have already dropped out of the race."

She nodded at a pickup truck that was pulling off the side of the road. A dispirited-looking guy sat up front. Bess and I grimaced when we saw the twisted, muddied bike frame that lay in the open truck bed.

"No wonder George is upset," Bess said. "Dropping out isn't her style. Or being disqualified. She's used to winning. She really needs us to be there for her. And instead we were talking about how tough the race has been for *Derek*."

Okay, I'll admit it. I felt pretty bad right then. "From now on, we're going to make sure George is our number-one priority," I said, more to myself than to Bess. "No matter what."

At each checkpoint, George looked more tired and stressed out. The good news was that she made it to every one before the cutoff time. Not much before, but at least she was still in the running. Bess and I made sure we had water and energy bars for her at every stop. And at the finish line for Stage One—in the western part of San Jose, the capital of Costa Rica—we did even more.

"George has a massage scheduled," Bess said, threading through the crowd that lined the street. She waved a small rectangle of paper under my nose, then slipped it into her bag. "All she has to do is show this appointment card when we get to the hotel."

The sun was low in the sky. Shadows were settling over the cement and stucco buildings that stretched along both sides of the avenue, and neon signs glowed in storefront windows. The street sloped downward, giving us a view of the sprawling city and mountains in the hazy distance.

"See her yet?" Bess asked. She fingered the strap of Paul's camera looped around her neck.

I shook my head. "The cutoff time is five fifteen," I said, checking my watch. "Just six minutes to go."

The top riders had finished long before. Bess and I hadn't seen them ourselves, since we'd been traveling at George's pace. But the crowd in San Jose was buzzing with the news when we got there. Derek had finished second, behind Juan Santiago. I was glad that he'd had such a strong finish, despite his accident, and that nothing else had gone wrong.

Nothing that we'd heard of, anyway.

"There!" Bess said, pointing down the road.

Five sweat-drenched and muddy cyclists were pedaling tiredly toward the finish line. I spotted George's yellow helmet in the middle of the pack. She was bent low over the handlebars, and it looked like she was struggling. Cheers rang out as she and the others rode over the finish line and came to a stop.

It was only then that George looked up.

"George!" Bess gasped.

Her face was twisted with pain. She looked as if she might fall off her bike. Bess and I pushed through the crowd and ran to her. As she got off her bicycle, she stumbled, clutching the calf of her right leg.

"Cramp . . . " she said, between clenched teeth.

I knelt down next to her and began to knead the rock-hard muscles. George groaned. Grabbing her water bottle, she took a long drink, and then removed her helmet and squirted water on her head.

"So . . . hot . . . ," she said.

"Well, you made it before cutoff, anyway," Bess said, smiling at her. "Can you eat anything?"

George took one look at the power bar in Bess's hand and shook her head. "Maybe later," she croaked out. She winced as I continued to rub the kinks out of her calf. "The last couple miles were murder," she said, beginning to find her voice. "My leg cramped up, but I knew I'd miss the cutoff if I stopped. . . . "

Twelve hours of off-road biking in hundred-degree heat had definitely gotten to her. She had to let Bess take her bike to the trucks carrying all the racers' bicycles to the hotel. Even with me supporting her, George had a hard time limping to our Jeep, and was so exhausted that she actually fell asleep during the drive to the hotel. Still, George is pretty amazing. One long, hot shower later, she was acting more like herself again.

"Air-conditioning . . . I love it!" she said, flopping down on her bed in clean shorts and a T-shirt. "I don't think I want to go out into that tropical heat ever again. Well, not for a while, anyway."

"Sorry you had such a hard day," I told her. "And

I'm really sorry if I did anything to make it worse."

George folded her arms under her head and stared thoughtfully up at the ceiling. "You were just trying to help Derek. And I was so hot and stressed out that maybe I overreacted a little," she said. "Now . . . didn't you guys say something about a massage?"

The people who had organized La Ruta had turned one of the hotel dining rooms into a makeshift spa. A woman at the door handed out robes and towels and directed people to the partitioned areas where the massage therapists worked. She pointed George toward one of the cubicles at the back.

"This is exactly what I need," she said. Taking a fluffy robe and towel from the woman at the door, she headed for the cubicle. "See you in an hour."

"We'll pick you up here," Bess called back to her.

As we left, I couldn't stop the thought that came into my head. "George won't need us until her massage is over," I said. "Which gives us an hour . . ."

"To try to figure out who sliced Derek's cable?" Bess stopped in the hallway to grin at me. "Face it, Nancy. You're hopelessly single-minded. I bet you haven't stopped thinking about what happened to Derek for a second."

"Guilty," I admitted. "I'm not going to let it stop me from being there for George. But stealing tools and slicing a brake cable is serious. We can't just let the person get away with it."

"Maybe we should find that mechanic, Miguel," Bess suggested.

"You read my mind," I told her.

Bess and I headed for the hotel lobby. When we'd arrived with George earlier, I'd noticed that one side of the lobby was cordoned off. Several mechanics had set up shop there, with benches, tools, and bike stands spread out around them. Muddied, battered bikes lined the walls. The whole area was a cluttered mess of tools and bikes and people. When we asked for Miguel, we were directed to a man taking a bike from the pile along the wall. He was older, with graying hair, a stubble of beard, and a belly that bulged under his work clothes.

"Miguel?" I said, stopping next to him.

"*Si?*" he asked. He had just finished clamping the bike onto his stand and was removing the front tire. Placing it on the floor, he glanced up at us. "Can I help you?"

"We're Derek McDaniel's friends," I told him. "You cleaned and adjusted his bike in Punta Leona before the race started, right?"

As soon as he heard Derek's name, Miguel sucked in his cheeks and frowned. "That is why I'm here. Many of the racers have hired me," he said.

He hadn't really answered my question. Had he avoided it on purpose?

"Someone cut his brake cable, you know," Bess pressed. "We're trying to help Derek figure out who did it."

"Derek told us you were the last person to work on the bike before the race," I added.

Miguel flashed an angry glance my way, then wiped his hands with a grease-stained rag. "I take excellent care of all the bikes," he said defensively. "Derek's was in perfect condition before the race. I took it myself to the *seguridad*."

"You mean the security truck?" Bess asked.

Miguel nodded.

"No one else touched the bike? You're sure?" I asked.

"*Ningún otro*. No one," he said firmly. He started to turn back to the bike he was working on, but then he paused. "Wait—I did leave the bike once. But it was for not longer than a few moments. There were some boys . . . *niños*. They were playing *futbal*—you know, soccer. They kicked their ball past the area where the other mechanics and I were working. They asked me to get it for them."

"Boys?" I turned to Bess, snapping my fingers. "Remember when we were at the restaurant in Punta Leona, right after Juan and his friends left?"

"Of course. He was playing soccer with a bunch of kids!" she said, nodding. "Do you think . . . ?"

"Excuse me," Miguel broke in. "I must have some room to do my work. . . . "

Bess and I got the message. Miguel obviously wasn't going to tell us anything more. We started to leave the mechanics' area.

"Do you think Juan asked those kids to kick that ball?" Bess said, under her breath. "You know, to make a distraction so he could slice the cable?"

"It makes sense—if Miguel is telling us the truth," I said. "I mean, he could be making up the story about the kids so that we don't suspect *him*. Juan, or anyone else, could have paid *him* to slice the cable."

"We can't exactly talk to the boys to confirm the story," Bess pointed out. "They're all the way back at Punta Leona."

"But we *can* talk to Juan," I said.

When you're a mystery hound like me, you tend to notice things—like the fact that Juan Santiago had set up a bike stand alongside the La Ruta mechanics. He was bent over his front wheel, using some kind of wrench on the spokes.

At that moment, Juan glanced up and saw us. I don't think I imagined the look of displeasure I saw in his eyes. He regarded us coolly as as we walked over to him.

"Did you hear about Derek's brake cable?" I asked him. "Someone sliced into it so it would snap during today's ride."

"So?" Juan shrugged and turned back to his bike. "If you don't mind, I am very busy."

Bess and I looked at each other. Maybe this guy was a top mountain-biker, but he wasn't going to get rid of us that easily. Not when Derek's safety was at stake—maybe even his life.

"This won't take long," Bess assured him. "Miguel says a couple of kids distracted him with their soccer ball yesterday, right after he finished tuning up Derek's bike."

"And we saw *you* playing soccer with them while we were having dinner last night," I added.

Juan's face remained stonily calm. "Kids look up to me. I like to play with them," he said.

He wasn't the most talkative guy in the world— not around us, anyway.

"I see the mechanics let you work in here with them," I went on. "Are you pretty good friends with Miguel?" The guy just shrugged, so I pushed it a little. "Good enough friends to get him to mess with Derek's brake cable?"

"You have a good imagination," Juan said. But he didn't laugh or smile. And when Bess and I tried asking more questions, his answers were short and didn't give anything away. I had to bite back my frustration when Bess and I left the mechanics' work area a few minutes later.

"Now what?" Bess wondered.

I glanced at the clock on the wall behind the reception desk. "We still have about twenty minutes before we have to meet George. Maybe we can—"

"Trust me, everything is going according to plan," a voice interrupted me.

It was so close and loud that Bess and I both whirled around. We didn't see anyone, but just behind us a recessed alcove angled sharply out of sight.

"The accident today was perfect," the smug voice went on.

"Nancy! Did you hear that?" Bess hissed.

I pressed my finger to my lips. The voice was definitely coming from that alcove. Bess's whispering made me miss part of what the person was saying, but the next words came through loud and clear.

"All the reports are saying the same thing," the voice went on. "That Derek McDaniel might wind up dead before La Ruta is over."

7

Friend—or Foe?

Bess and I flew around the corner and into the alcove. "What did you say?" I asked, then stopped short.

"Cynthia?"

Derek's agent stood next to a counter that ran along one side of the alcove. The counter was covered with papers from Cynthia's briefcase, and pay phones dotted the wall above. Instead of using a pay phone, Cynthia had her ear glued to her cell phone. Seeing me, she half frowned.

"That's right," she said into her phone. "With all the new press, Aqua Trim will have to up their offer or they're out of the running. . . . Oh—can you hang on for a sec?"

She glanced impatiently at Bess and me. "Derek's

friends, right?" she said. Not that she gave us a second to answer. "I'm a little busy now, girls. Is there something you want?"

"Just a couple of answers. We'll wait," I said.

I guess Cynthia got the message that we weren't going to go away. She got off the phone and turned to us with a thin smile. "What's up?" she asked.

My mind was swimming with thoughts—none of them very flattering to Cynthia. After what we'd just heard, I wondered just how far she would go to get the best endorsement deal possible for Derek.

"We, uh, couldn't help hearing what you said," I began. "You know, about a plan, and that Derek might wind up dead. Do you know something we don't about what happened today?"

"Or about a plan for another attack on him?" Bess asked.

"Really, girls, you can't take things so seriously," Cynthia said, with a dismissive wave. "It was just a figure of speech. Nobody's going to die."

"But . . . what did you mean when you said everything's going according to plan?" I asked.

Cynthia tucked her blond hair behind her ears and frowned at us. "You obviously don't understand the advertising business," she said. "Take a look at this newscast."

She touched a series of keys on her cell phone,

then held it out so we could see the screen. Before long, a sports newscast appeared. Through the phone's speaker, we heard the anchorman say something about the ultimate mountain-biking race and high drama in the Costa Rican rain forest.

"He must be talking about Derek's brake cable!" Bess said.

Then the image on the screen switched to an interview, and we were looking at a tiny image of Derek—mud-splattered, breathless, and sweaty—talking to a reporter right next to the finish line for Stage One.

"Sure, the sabotage was a blow," Derek was saying. "But I pulled through with a strong ride, and . . . "

He tried to talk about the race, but the reporter kept interrupting with more questions about the sliced cable and who Derek thought was out to stop him. Cynthia pulled up three other sportscasts. They, too, featured stories about Derek that played up the sabotage.

"Ever since the story broke, my phone hasn't stopped ringing," Cynthia said, practically bursting with glee. "Two new companies are interested in signing Derek for endorsement deals. The numbers just keep getting bigger. That sliced cable is the best thing that ever happened to Derek."

"How can you say that? He could have been hurt!" Bess said.

"But he wasn't. And the publicity is making him wildly attractive to companies looking for athletes to publicize their products," Cynthia said. A smug smile spread across her face as she gathered papers together and slipped them into her briefcase. "Thanks to that accident, all my hard work is finally paying off."

With that, she snapped her briefcase shut, nodded curtly at Bess and me, and was gone. For a moment, we just stood there staring after her.

"All her hard work? What did she mean by that?" Bess said. "She wouldn't sabotage her own client, would she?"

"It's hard to imagine anyone doing that. I mean, it wouldn't be very good for business if Derek got hurt and couldn't mountain-bike anymore," I said, trying to think it out. "Still, Cynthia has probably been at other races, so she could be the one who slipped him those notes. She might have been hoping he'd go to the press with them."

I didn't like what I was thinking, but it made sense in a twisted way. "Maybe she figured an experienced biker like Derek wouldn't get seriously hurt, even with a snapped brake cable," I said. "Maybe she decided it was worth the chance, since the extra publicity could mean a bigger endorsement deal."

"Yuck." Bess shook her head in disgust. "Shouldn't we say something to Derek?"

I had been wondering the same thing, but I wasn't sure it was a great idea. "Derek trusts Cynthia. It might really blow his concentration if he thinks his own agent was the one who sabotaged his bike," I said. "Anyway, Juan is still a big suspect too. We'll just have to keep an eye on both of them and do everything we can to make sure Derek finishes the race without any more attacks."

Our hour was almost up, so Bess and I headed back to the massage area to pick up George. We reached it just as she came out. She looked like a new person. Her face was glowing, and she seemed totally relaxed. There wasn't a trace of stiffness in her walk.

"Marta really knows how to get the kinks out," George said, grinning at us. "It took an hour of being pummeled and kneaded, but I'm starting to feel like I'll be able to handle tomorrow's ride." She opened her mouth to say something more, but the words were swallowed by a giant-size yawn. "All I need now is about sixty hours of sleep."

"Dinner first," Bess insisted. "You're going to need the extra calories tomorrow."

"That's for sure," George agreed. "Stage Two is the hardest part of La Ruta. We're going to ride to the top of the Irazú volcano. And going down is supposed to be even worse."

I had read about Irazú in the race pamphlet. Actually, Irazú and another volcano, Turrialba, were part of a range of connected peaks. The race course crossed both volcanoes, and riding them was supposed to be La Ruta's ultimate challenge.

"Hopefully it's not as bad as it sounds," I said.

Since George was so tired, we decided to have dinner at the hotel restaurant instead of going out. George's eyes were drooping, but she managed to pack it in anyway. She ordered beef and vegetable soup and a couple of tortilla sandwiches called *gallos*. I guess she realized how hungry she was, because she picked at my chicken with rice and had a bit of Bess's pork empanada. She even got a sweet, milky rice pudding sprinkled with cinnamon to finish off the meal, while Bess and I shared a flan. By the time we left the restaurant, all three of us were totally stuffed—and George wasn't the only one yawning. No big surprise, since we'd gotten up a couple hours before dawn.

"Would you guys mind stopping at Sharine's room?" George asked, heading for the hotel desk. "She pulled ahead of me when I got my leg cramp. I want to find out how she finished today."

Sharine and Derek both had rooms on the third floor, so we took the elevator up. "Looks like room 315 is this way," Bess said, heading left down the hall. "That's Sharine's room, right?"

"Yup. And the guy at the desk said Derek's is 307," George said. "Hey! Isn't that them?"

She nodded toward an open doorway halfway down the hall. Sure enough, Derek and Sharine stood just inside it, with their backs to us.

"Hi, you two!" Bess called.

Neither of them answered, or even turned around. Weird, I thought. As we got closer, I saw that Derek held a sheet of paper. He and Sharine were staring at it with shocked, fearful eyes.

"Oh, no," I said. "Don't tell me...."

Derek held out the paper so I could read the words that had been written across it in jagged block letters: *I CAN GET TO YOU AGAIN—ANYTIME, ANYWHERE.*

8

Deadly Words

'm not sure how long we stood there gaping at that note. The air around us seemed to buzz with tension, until at last Sharine broke the silence.

"This is the third note. We found it on the floor when we opened Derek's door just now," she said, in a hollow voice. "And after what happened today, we know he means it."

"Or she," I said. "It could be a woman who cut your brake cable."

Derek shook his head. "Why would a woman choose to threaten *me*?" he wondered out loud. "There are half a dozen other guys who are serious competitors at the top of the racing circuit. Why not one of them?"

I decided not to mention that the woman I was

thinking of was Cynthia. Luckily, Sharine changed the subject so I didn't have to explain.

"What about Juan?" she asked. "He's the one who moved into first place after Derek wiped out."

"Bess and I talked to him," I said. "He's not exactly your biggest fan, Derek, but we still don't have any proof that he sliced your cable or wrote any threatening notes. Do you remember whether he was at those two races back in the States?"

"The ones where someone slipped me those other notes?" He tapped the paper with his forefinger, then shrugged. "I'm just not sure. I don't remember him being a top contender, but I guess he might have been there."

"What about Cynthia?" Bess piped up. "Does she go to all your races?"

"Most of them," Derek said. "But what does that have to do with anything?"

Next to me, George was leaning against the frame of the door to Derek's room. "Guys?" she said tiredly. "I know it was my idea to come here, but I don't think I can stay awake much longer."

"We all need to get some rest. We're going to need it," said Sharine. Smiling at George, she asked, "Do you still want to ride together? I'm going to need the moral support when we head up Irazú."

"Me, too," George said.

"And don't worry," Bess added. "Nancy and I will keep an extra-close watch to make sure whoever wrote that note doesn't have a chance to make good on the threat."

"Can you believe it? We're actually at the top of a volcano," Bess said, late the next morning. "This part of Costa Rica is amazing!"

That was for sure. Here at the peak of Irazú, we stood among the bare craggy rocks surrounding the crater. Lush green coffee farms spread out over the hillside below us. Through a hazy mist of volcanic ash, we saw a blanket of clouds nestled against the hills.

"It *is* beautiful," I agreed, watching Bess snap photos with the camera Paul had lent her. "I just hope George has enough layers to keep warm. I mean, I knew the temperature would drop here on top of the volcano. But this feels like February back home, not like the tropics."

I wasn't sure when I had started to shiver. Stage Two of the race had already been under way for hours. During our drive up the volcano we'd seen sloths, iguanas, and even a couple of crocodiles. Derek, George, and Sharine had all come through the first checkpoint in good form. Derek had been at the front of the lead pack of riders, and George and Sharine had reached the checkpoint well before the cutoff.

But conditions started getting tougher after that. As we'd climbed higher, the wind had picked up and the temperature had dropped. George and Sharine had both stopped to pull on sweatshirts. Then the race path had turned off into a single, washed-out muddy track that rose up into the cloud forest. Bess and I hadn't seen George or Sharine since. Now we hovered alongside journalists and other support crews next to the La Ruta truck that marked the second checkpoint.

"Well, moving around taking pictures is helping me not to freeze," Bess said. She swung her camera around to get a shot of two boys leading some cows along the dirt track.

"I see you've discovered one of the secret benefits of photography," Paul Maynard said, turning away from the crowd of reporters. He snapped a few shots of us, then grinned at Bess over the top of his camera. "Being in constant motion definitely keeps the blood flowing so you stay warm."

His cheeks were flushed, but I thought that was probably from being around Bess, not from taking photos.

"Thanks again for lending me your camera," Bess said, smiling back at him. "I've been having a blast with it."

As Paul stepped over to us, I realized that he had on cycling clothes instead of his usual Hawaiian shirt and baggy shorts. When I asked him why, he grinned and said, "I decided it's time to get some inside shots of this race. I hired someone to drive my car to the next checkpoint, so I can be in the thick of the pack while they head down Irazú," he said, speaking above the wind that whistled around us.

Paul nodded toward his muddy car. I saw that a rack had been strapped to the trunk and a mountain bike hung from it. A young man with dark, spiked hair leaned against the side door with his arms crossed over his chest.

"You're going to ride?" I asked. "What about your injury—the one that made you give up racing?"

"I'm not trying to *win* the race, just get pictures of it. If I ride carefully, I'll be all right," Paul said. He nodded at the camera Bess held. "Actually, I was hoping you'd take some photos of me when I get to the next checkpoint."

"Sure," Bess told him. "But only if you help me look over the shots I've taken and pick out the best ones."

"Deal." Paul turned to look over his shoulder as people around us started whistling and clapping. "Looks like the first riders are here. *Carlos! La bicicleta, por favor!*"

Paul was all action, moving out onto the trail with

71

his camera ready. As I gazed down the cow track, I felt my muscles tighten. Whoever had slipped that note under Derek's door had said he could get to Derek anytime, anywhere. . . . The nervous butterflies in my stomach made it so that I hardly felt the cold anymore. Time seemed to be moving in slow motion. It felt like forever before Derek finally rode up to the checkpoint.

"Yes!" I cheered, along with the crowd.

Derek was so out of breath that he couldn't speak at first. He kept glancing over his shoulder as he reached for a sandwich, without even getting off his bike. When someone offered him a sports drink, he shook his head.

"T-tea," he said between chattering teeth. "Something to w-warm me up."

I guess the race organizers had known what to expect. In addition to serving sandwiches and sports drinks, the people in the La Ruta service truck kept two pots of sugarcane tea simmering on a hot plate. A few seconds later, Derek was dipping his sandwich into a steaming mug and eating the moistened pieces. Reporters crowded around him, pelting him with questions.

"Any more attacks, Derek?"

"Is the threat of being targeted affecting your concentration?

"Do you think you can win?"

I was starting to think the reporters were as big a threat to Derek's concentration as anyone. "Everything's great," was all he said. "If you'll excuse me . . ."

He didn't stick around to chat. Not that I blamed him. He had to finish Stage Two well ahead of Juan if he hoped to beat his overall time and move into first place. As he rode past me, he gave an anxious smile. "So far, so good," he said. "Let's hope my luck holds out."

It was a full five minutes before Juan rode up. Like Derek, he stayed only long enough to drink some tea.

"Here's where I head off too," Paul said, as Juan continued on the path that would go down the other side of the volcano. Paul got on his mountain bike. He wore a special helmet—one that had a harness attached for his camera. A thin wire stretched from the camera to his index finger—I figured that would let him take pictures without letting go of the handlebars. With a wave to Bess and me, he was off. His ponytail dangled below his helmet as he headed down the track behind Juan.

After that, riders started coming fast and furious. Bess flew around taking pictures—mostly of freezing cold racers gulping down tea and trying to eat. Bess and I were really glad when George and Sharine reached the checkpoint over half an hour before the cutoff time.

"This r-race is nuts," George said, curling her hands around the cup of tea I got for her. "Yesterday, people dropped out because of heat and dehydration. Today . . . n-no one can get w-warm."

"But you're still in the race," Bess pointed out. "Not to mention that I got some great shots of you both with the clouds and coffee farms in the background. Paul gave me some tips on how to get the best camera angles. He's going to help me pick out the best shots, too."

"S-sounds like you have a fan," Sharine teased, shivering through her smile. "Just b-be sure to send me copies so I can remember how freezing cold and miserable I feel right now," she said.

Even though she and George couldn't seem to stop shaking, two cups of tea and a sandwich later, they felt warm enough to ride on toward the next checkpoint.

Not that it was easy to get there. Our Jeep couldn't follow the race trail—a rutted path of loose rocks and dirt. But the road we took didn't seem much better. Dry ground turned to ashy mud as soon as we got below the clouds. We passed two trucks that were buried up to the tops of their tires in the gooey muck. Besides which, we kept having to circle around cows that shared the road with us. I'm not sure how we didn't get stuck ourselves, but somehow we made it to the third checkpoint.

"Looks like the first riders have already come through," Bess said, as we pulled off the side of the road just beyond the La Ruta service truck.

A group of four riders came bouncing over the rocky mud toward the checkpoint. I didn't see Derek or Juan among them.

"Has Derek McDaniel come through already?" I asked one of the people in the La Ruta service truck. "Or Juan Santiago?"

The guy nodded as he handed sports drinks and hot tea to the racers who had just arrived. "Sure. About fifteen minutes ago. Derek came through first, but Juan was right on his tail," he said.

"What about Paul Maynard?" Bess asked. "He's a journalist but he's riding to get photos."

The guy in the truck rolled his eyes. "Yeah, he came through too," he told us. "He was so busy taking photos that he nearly went headfirst into that fence."

Bess grimaced at the barbed wire that ran along the vine-covered shrubs and trees edging the road. "I can't believe I didn't get here in time to take pictures of him. I mean, he's been so nice. I don't want to disappoint him."

I couldn't help smiling at that. "I'm pretty sure he'll forgive you. Anyway, you can get some pictures of him at today's finish," I suggested.

The butterflies in my stomach were finally starting to calm themselves. We'd made it three-quarters of the way through the day's course, and Derek was still fine. We'd been so busy that we hadn't had time to follow up on the note—or do anything more to look into the sliced cable and missing tool kit. Juan was racing, so I couldn't talk to him. But . . .

"Have you seen Cynthia today?" I asked Bess.

She lowered her camera. "No. Now that you mention it, I haven't seen her all day."

"Weird," I said. "You'd think she'd want to see how Derek was doing, since she has that big Aqua Trim deal in the works."

I was still thinking about it when Sharine rode up. I got nervous all over again when I saw the serious, urgent expression on her face.

"It's George . . . ," Sharine said breathlessly, squeezing on the brakes. "She's hurt."

9

Crash Landing

Hurt!" Bess and I cried at the same time.

"Where? How? What happened?" Bess asked.

Sharine was covered with mud. The muscles in her face were tight, and her knuckles were white from gripping the brakes. She was shivering, and the raw wind whipping around us probably wasn't helping. As she got off her bicycle, she gestured back up the rocky trail.

"She's a couple miles up," Sharine told us. "Her tires slipped on the loose rocks, and then she crashed into a boulder. She's got a gash on her shoulder, and I think maybe she hurt her ankle, too."

I tried to push aside the grim picture that had formed in my mind. "We have to help her!" I said.

But one look up that steep, rocky trail and I knew we wouldn't make it in our Jeep. "We'll go on foot."

Bess was already running toward the first-aid tent. Two guys came out with a first-aid kit and a stretcher, and we set off up the trail. Bikes hurtled down the steep hill toward us, skidding on the loose rocks.

"Hey! Isn't that George?" I pointed at a rider hunched over so that we could only see the top of a yellow helmet. It *was* George, peddling slowly. Bikes veered wildly around her as they careened toward the checkpoint. My stomach bottomed out when I saw the red stain that was spreading across the shoulder of her muddy biking jersey.

"Oh, my gosh!" Bess breathed.

She and I sprinted ahead. When George looked up, I saw scratches on her face. She slowed her bike to a stop just as Bess and I reached her, followed by the two first-aid workers.

"Sharine told us what happened," I said, taking her bike while Bess helped her to sit on the rocks at the edge of the trail. "Where are you hurt?"

George managed a small smile. "Everywhere. But I guess my shoulder is the worst," she said. She winced as the first-aid guys gingerly widened the blood-stained rip in her jersey so they could examine the cut beneath. "I thought I sprained my ankle, but it doesn't feel so bad now."

Bess and I helped to untie her biking shoe and take off her sock. For the next ten minutes, the first-aid workers checked her out from head to toe. They cleaned and bandaged the cut on George's shoulder and covered up the worst cuts on her arms, legs, and forehead.

While they worked, I looked over her bike. After what had happened to Derek's brake cable, I wanted to make sure George's bike hadn't been tampered with. Especially since Miguel was her mechanic too. From what I could tell, her cable, chain, and brakes were all okay.

"Your bike seems to be in working order," I reported. "How are *you* doing?"

One of the first-aid workers, an American guy with close-shaved dark hair, was wrapping George's ankle with an Ace bandage. "As soon as I'm done here, she's good to go," he told me.

"She can keep racing?" Bess asked. "Are you sure that's a good idea?"

"Your friend twisted her ankle, but it's not sprained," said the first-aid worker. Turning to George, he added, "Just try not to stress it any more than you have to. We'll want to see that cut again at the end of the race, but the bleeding's stopped. If you want to ride, no one's going to stop you."

"I want to," George said, as she retied her shoe. "That's what I came for, after all."

I wasn't sure it was a great idea for George to push herself to finish Stage Two. But she *had* asked us to cheer her on, no matter what. And if the first-aid workers said she was good to go, then maybe she wasn't in such bad shape.

Still, George was pretty quiet while we walked with her to the service truck and got tea and some rice and beans to eat. Sharine had already continued down toward the finish line for Stage Two. Other riders were making quick stops to warm up and change brake pads that were worn out from the steep, rocky descent. We watched a dozen racers come and go before George finally reached for her bike.

"I guess I'll go now," she said. She gave a bittersweet laugh. "Anyway, nothing could be worse than crashing into a boulder. What more could go wrong?" she said.

And then she rode on down the trail. I have to admit, I was impressed. No one on the planet had more determination and guts than George. But I was worried, too.

"Uh-oh," Bess said, angling a look up at the sky as we ran to our Jeep to follow.

I had noticed it too—the dark bank of clouds that was starting to blot out the sun.

Splat. As we started down the trail, the first heavy drops fell onto our windshield. We barely had time to roll up the windows before the rain started pouring down. Within seconds, George was totally drenched.

Past the checkpoint, the race route joined the road that the support teams had been driving on. It was hard to see through the wall of rain, but it looked like a brown, muddy lake. I was worried for George, but she just rode ahead with a grim, determined look on her face. All around her, riders slipped and got stuck in the endless puddles. I gripped the steering wheel tighter as the Jeep dipped down into wet mud that sucked at our tires.

"Well, now we know what else could go wrong," I said. "If this rain keeps up, it'll be a miracle if *any* of us get to today's finish line."

Luckily for us, weather in tropical places like Costa Rica can change in an instant. After about half an hour, the downpour stopped as suddenly as it had started. Sunlight glared off our wet windshield. As we passed through a village, Bess took some photos of rain-soaked kids that waved and called out in Spanish while they splashed in the puddles alongside the road.

George, riding next to us, didn't even seem to notice the kids. Her face was tight and serious, and she rode hunched over the handlebars. When the race route turned onto yet another washed-out gully, George got off her bike, heaved it onto her uninjured shoulder, and hiked down the trail away from us.

"Did you see that, Nancy? She barely looked up when you beeped good-bye," Bess said, biting her lip. "I know George told us she wants to finish no matter what, but I'm worried."

"Me, too," I admitted.

I was definitely feeling anxious again. I pressed a little harder on the gas. All of a sudden, I wanted to get to the finish line. Not that getting there sooner would help George. But I guess her accident made me worry about how Derek was doing too.

I wasn't sure when the rocky downhill trail shifted from Irazú to the Turrialba volcano. To me, it all looked insanely rough—full of slippery rocks and ditches. As we got farther down, the road snaked back and forth in a series of sharp curves. We began to see more trucks and ATVs, and then I saw a handful of bikers turning onto the road from a rutted trail.

"Check it out! It looks like we're just in time to see the top racers finish," Bess said. "Isn't that Derek?"

Bess pointed at the biker who led the pack. "Yes!" I crowed when I saw his neon-green helmet.

But then I spotted another racer disappearing around a hairpin curve *ahead* of Derek. "Uh-oh. Derek's lost the lead," I murmured.

The road was so clogged with trucks and ATVs that it took a while to drive down the last few hairpin turns to the end of Stage Two. Like the day before, there was a huge crowd. Cameras flashed, and people stood three deep on both sides of the road. By the time we parked our Jeep, Derek was already being mobbed by reporters. I couldn't hear every word they said, but what I *did* hear made me worry.

"Not the strongest finish . . ."

"Third place overall. How do you feel about that, Derek?"

"You had such a strong start. How did you veer off course?"

An alarm went off inside my head when I heard that. "Derek veered off course?" I said to Bess. "But there are markers all over the place."

Derek was mumbling something about a misplaced marker. I didn't see Cynthia standing next to him until she stepped in front and cut him off.

"That marker wasn't misplaced," Cynthia said, shaking her head dramatically. "Someone moved it on purpose!"

10

Tricks on the Trail

Y ou can bet *that* got a reaction from reporters. Everyone wanted to know *who* had moved the marker.

"I'm not a detective," Cynthia said, holding up a hand to quiet the reporters. "But it's clear to me that other racers feel that cheating is the only way to stop Derek from winning. . . ."

"Did you hear that?" Bess said, her eyes wide.

We tried to get closer to Derek and Cynthia. No such luck. A wall of reporters, hungry for Derek's story, blocked our way. It was like we were just outside a whirlwind of questions and snapping cameras. Talk about frustrating. All Bess and I could do was wait until the reporters finally surged toward another racer at the finish line.

"Derek!" I said, hurrying over to him. "What happened?"

Derek scowled as he peeled off his biking gloves. "Someone moved one of the race markers," he said. "I rode down the trail for half a mile before I realized I was going the wrong way." He shook his head in disgust and kicked some of the mud from his shoes. "It cost me the lead in the race."

"You're sure it was moved?" I asked. "I mean, is it possible that you just misread it and went the wrong way by mistake?"

"No way," Derek said firmly. "On the way back, I found four other people who'd followed the same marker. We all had to turn around and retrace our path to the real trail. One of the race officials was fixing the marker when we got there. He told us it was definitely in the wrong place. Someone had to have moved it."

So many possibilities swirled in my head. I wasn't sure what to think. Over by the finish line, Cynthia gestured dramatically while she spoke Could *she* have found a way to move that marker? Then, there was Juan. . . .

"Where's Juan Santiago?" I asked, scanning the crowd.

Derek's scowl deepened. "Juan? He came through ten minutes ahead of me to finish first," he said. "That's what the reporters told me, anyway. He's probably on his way to the hotel by now."

"You think *he* moved the marker?" Bess said.

"Maybe, but what about Miguel? Do you think he could be involved?" I asked, thinking out loud. Not that Derek had any answer for me. He just shrugged.

"We need to talk to someone else who was on the race course. Like maybe that official who moved the marker back to its right place. Do you see him around anywhere?" I asked.

Derek peered at the cluster of people who stood near the finish line. A bunch of them were wearing La Ruta staff jerseys. "Sorry," he said, shaking his head. "I barely even glanced at the guy. All I wanted to do was get back in the race."

"Maybe we could talk to some of the other racers?" I suggested. "Or—"

"What about Paul?" Bess pointed to the finish line. Paul was pedaling up with his camera in its special harness. He looked just as muddy and out of breath as the other mountain-bikers. While he took photographs of the other racers, Bess ran over to snap some shots of *him*.

Paul was so winded that he couldn't say much until after he had had half a bottle of water. But he still managed a grin while he walked his bike over to where Bess and I stood.

"Man, what a workout. My whole body aches," he told us. "It was worth it, though. I almost forgot I was there to take pictures, and not racing to win myself." Paul peered toward Derek, who was wheeling his bicycle toward the La Ruta security truck. "I managed to keep up with the great Derek McDaniel for a while. I got some great shots."

"Shots?" I blinked at him as an idea hit me. "Do you think we could take a look at them?" I asked.

Paul was in the middle of unstrapping his harness and removing the camera from it. "Hmm?" he said, looking distractedly around. "Carlos should be around here somewhere. . . . "

"The photos," Bess pressed. "Something happened up on the volcano. A marker was moved. We thought maybe you saw it—or got a picture of it."

Paul had spotted Carlos standing next to his car farther down the road. But I guess what we were saying finally got through to him. He stopped looking all over the place and zeroed in on us with a hundred percent of his attention.

"A marker was moved? On purpose?" he asked.

Bess and I told him what had happened. While he listened, his gaze flickered once more to where Derek was handing his mountain bike over to the security truck.

"So Derek's in third place now, huh?" he said, when we were done. "There's only one day left. It's going to be tough for him to make up enough time to win La Ruta."

"Especially if whoever moved that marker does something *else* to sabotage him," Bess said. "But winning the race isn't the only thing to worry about. Derek could be in danger."

"Which is why we want to see your photos," I added.

Paul's gaze flickered to us again, and he nodded. "Sure. You're welcome to take a look if you think it will help," he agreed. "I kept pretty close to Derek and Juan for most of the ride down the volcano."

That was music to my ears. "Did you see anyone messing with a marker?" I asked.

"Were there any mechanics on the race course?" Bess added. "Like maybe that guy Miguel?"

Paul rubbed his chin for a moment, then shook his head. "Not that I noticed. But like you say, maybe my camera saw something that I missed. I can download the pictures right now."

Walking his bike, Paul made his way through the crowd to his car, which was parked off the side of the road a couple hundred feet back. Carlos leaned against the driver's-side door with his arms crossed over his chest. After handing over the car keys, he took the money Paul gave him and sauntered over to the crowd at the finish line.

"Step into my office," Paul joked. He opened the car door and pushed the driver's seat forward so Bess and I could climb in back. Bulky carrying cases formed a messy mound on the passenger seat, and some empty water bottles and candy wrappers lay on the floor. Paul unzipped one of the cases, pulled a laptop computer and cable from it, and squeezed in next to Bess and me in the back. Minutes later, the photographs were downloaded and we were scrolling through them.

"Hmm," I said, looking at each picture as it appeared on the screen. There were a couple shots of Derek wading through muddy water up to his waist while rain beat down on him. There were some of Juan and another rider, sending sprays of mud out from their tires as they bumped over the rocks in a gully the rain had washed out. There were dozens more—bikers crashing, bikers digging their heels against the gravel and rocks on steep hills, people clapping and waving from tiny villages along the race route.

"Wait—can you go back to that last shot?" I asked.

Paul clicked the mouse, and a photo of the lush green Costa Rican rain forest flashed onto the screen. Some cinder-block houses with corrugated metal roofs were clustered close to the trail. Juan Santiago had stopped and stood straddling his bike while a group of boys and girls clamored around him.

"He's giving out money," Bess said.

I had already noticed the coins in Juan's outstretched hand. "The question is, why?" I wondered.

"You think he might have paid them to move that race route marker?" Paul asked. His eyes narrowed as he took a second look at the photo. "Now that you mention it, this was pretty far down the volcano. I'm not sure where that marker was moved, but it could have been nearby."

Hmm. I was starting to see a pattern—one that troubled me. "Think about it. Back in Punta Leona, Juan was talking to some kids right before they distracted Miguel with their soccer ball," I said. "And now we see a photo of Juan with more kids. . . ."

"Who might have moved that marker to throw Derek off the right trail!" Bess finished. She scowled at the computer screen. "Paying little kids to do his dirty work . . . That's really low."

"If that's what happened. We don't know for sure yet," I reminded her. "Do you have a printer, Paul? It would be great if you could print a copy for us to show Derek. He ought to be able to tell us if this village is close to the marker that was moved."

"No problem. I can make a copy for you when I get to the hotel," Paul said. "But I'll be here for a while taking photos of the riders—the ones that are left, that is. I heard one of the race organizers say over seventy people have dropped out so far."

"Wow. I hope George isn't one of them," Bess said.

I was thinking about George too, but there wasn't anything we could do except wait for her. We scrolled through the rest of the photographs, but Bess and I didn't see anything else that might help us figure out who had moved the marker. A few minutes later, we climbed out of Paul's car and headed back toward the finish line.

Paul immediately jumped to the front of the crowd to take pictures. "Don't forget," he called back to Bess. "We have a date to download your photos later, okay?"

Bess nodded, but I don't think he saw. His eye was already glued to his camera. As more and more racers arrived, I saw faces that drooped with fatigue and bikes that were even more battered and muddy than the day before. We didn't see George among them. We waited—and waited. Even after the sun sank behind the volcanoes, George hadn't appeared.

"She's going to miss the cutoff," Bess said, biting her lip. "There are just two minutes left and—"

At that moment, we caught sight of her. George was pedaling slowly. As she rode beneath a street light, I saw that she was plastered with mud. Through the grime I spotted a blotch of pinkish-red on her shoulder.

"Her cut . . . It's still bleeding!" Bess gasped.

George's face was tight with pain—her eyes were slits in her mud-covered face. No sooner did she cross the finish line than she stumbled. Her bike fell to the ground with a crash.

"George!" I cried.

As Bess and I leaped toward her, George collapsed in a heap on the pavement.

11

Going Too Far

"Oh my gosh," Bess breathed. "Someone help us!"

She and I dropped down next to George, who lay on her side on the ground. Her eyes fluttered open. "Oooh . . . ," she groaned, trying to sit up.

"Take it easy," I cautioned.

A couple of first-aid workers appeared with a stretcher. I recognized one of them—the guy with close-shaved dark hair who had helped George after her crash on Irazú. As he kneeled down next to George, he smiled and said, "You, again? We've got to stop meeting like this."

"That's . . . for . . . sure," she croaked out, between gasping breaths.

"Is she going to be all right?" Bess asked.

He and the other first-aid worker were already

helping George onto the stretcher. "We'll give her a thorough exam. But it looks to me like she probably just needs a fresh bandage and some liquids in her system," he said.

"Not to mention a hot shower, a massage, and about three days of sleep," Bess added.

The dark-haired guy laughed. Nodding at the other first-aid worker, he said, "Lydia and I can take care of the bandage and liquids. We'll leave the rest to you."

"Did I . . . make it before . . . the cutoff?" George asked, lifting her head to gaze worriedly at Bess and me.

"With about thirty seconds to spare," I said, nodding.

George gave a small smile, but I couldn't share it. I mean, was it worth it to stay in the competition if she collapsed at the end of every day?

I hadn't noticed before, but the first-aid tent was a real hot spot. There were so many people that Bess and I had to wait outside for George. We must have seen a couple dozen riders limping in—or getting carried in on stretchers like George. A lot of them weren't as lucky as she was, though. They'd had to drop out of the race or hadn't finished before the cutoff time.

It was totally dark by the time George came out of the tent, with a fresh bandage and wearing a clean T-shirt they'd found for her. She walked stiffly and looked more exhausted than I'd ever seen her, but the medical attendants hadn't found anything seriously wrong.

"They say I'm okay to ride tomorrow . . . if I want to," George said, climbing tiredly into the backseat of our Jeep.

Bess shot me a worried glance from the passenger seat. "*Do* you want to?" she asked George.

George didn't answer right away. She let out a deep sigh and stared out the window. We were heading toward our hotel, in the town of Turrialba, at the foot of the Irazú and Turrialba volcanoes. We'd seen it from the finish line before the sun had set—a grid of streets and buildings that sat in a gorgeous river valley. In the daylight, the volcanoes had towered over us, clouded with steam and ash. Now that darkness had fallen, it was the lights from the town that we noticed, twinkling across the valley like a carpet of stars.

"I'd be crazy *not* to finish . . . I guess," George said at last.

It sounded to me like George's resolve was cracking—a little, anyway. "You've ridden incredibly hard, George," I told her. "You made it through Stage Two even after you got hurt. Whether or not you ride tomorrow, you should be totally proud of yourself."

George gave a shrug—not the most convincing sign of confidence.

I had been reading street signs while I talked. You see, I don't always have the best luck behind the wheel. Bess and George have stopped trying to keep track of the number of times I've run out of gas or gotten lost because my mind was on a case. But this time, luck was with me. As we got closer to the center of Turrialba, I saw that the streets were numbered. The one we were looking for was right off the main square—a green park with a starburst of paths that spread out from a gazebo at its center. Our hotel was just half a block away.

"Over there. The Hotel Buena Vista," Bess said, pointing at a three-story stucco building. "That's the place."

"It's smaller than where we stayed yesterday," I said. "There can't possibly be enough room for all the racers."

"La Ruta has people staying in hotels all over the city," Bess said, pulling a pamphlet from her bag. "Race officials are at a place called the Hotel Del Rio. It's pretty close to here, next to some big river that runs through the town."

"The Turrialba River. The white-water rafting there is supposed to be unbelievable," George said tiredly from the backseat. She moved her shoulder stiffly, wincing a little. "Not that I'll be able to check it out anytime soon."

"Don't worry about that," Bess told her. "Don't

worry about anything until after you've had a steaming hot bubble bath."

"If you say so," George said. She leaned her head against the seat and closed her eyes. "But what about . . . ?"

"Nancy and I will take care of everything," Bess assured her. "We'll make sure Miguel gives your bike a major tune-up."

"I want to talk to him anyway," I added. "We need to find out if he had anything to do with that marker being moved."

George's eyes fluttered open. "Marker?" she asked. Then she closed her eyes again. "Oh, I'm soooo tired."

"Don't worry about it," Bess put in, with a warning look at me. I knew what she meant: George needed to rest now, not worry about the attacks on Derek. "I'm not sure where the massages are—probably over at the Del Rio, since that's where race officials are staying," Bess went on. "Nancy and I will check it out while you take a bath."

George moved slowly as she got out of the Jeep. "I don't know, guys," she said, half frowning. "What I could really use is . . . "

Her words were swallowed by a huge yawn.

"Some rest?" Bess finished for her. "Don't worry. That's part of our plan."

It was more clear than ever that George had pushed

herself beyond her limit. She took stiff, limping steps. She hardly said a word while we checked in, found our room, and got a bath ready for her.

"You'll probably feel better after soaking in there for a while," I said, nodding through the bathroom doorway at the bubble-filled tub. "Bess and I will be back after we schedule the massage."

"Sure, okay," she said flatly. The same brooding frown stayed on her face as she headed for the bathroom and shut the door behind her.

Bess and I didn't say anything until we were in the hall outside our room. "I know George told us to help her finish no matter what, but pushing her doesn't seem like the right thing to do," Bess said. "Not after all she's been through today."

"That's for sure. But it's up to her," I said. "We need to be there for her whether she finishes or not."

I have to admit, I was eager to get over to the Hotel Del Rio—and not just to schedule George's massage. Between the threatening notes, the stolen tool kit, the sliced brake cable, and now the marker, the attacks on Derek just kept coming. We hadn't had a chance to show Derek the photograph Paul had taken of Juan giving money to kids along the race route. If that village *was* near the place where the marker was moved, it was more likely than ever that Juan was the person we were trying to stop.

I took a deep breath, trying to clear my head. It was a cool evening, but the air had lost its sharp bite now that we were off the volcanoes. Lots of people strolled along the streets and on the walks in the town park. In the yellow glare of the street lamps, we saw a crowd of kids kicking a soccer ball on one of the grassy lawns near the gazebo.

"Hey—isn't that Juan Santiago?" Bess said.

She pointed toward the kids, and I saw a taller figure among them. Yup, it was Juan, all right. The kids flocked eagerly around him, chattering a mile a minute in Spanish.

"He looks innocent enough . . . ," I murmured.

"That's what he wants everyone to think," Bess said. As we passed by him, she scowled and called out, "Hey, Juan! What are you doing now? Convincing a new bunch of kids to do your dirty work for you?"

Juan trapped the ball with his foot and turned to look at us. "Excuse me?" he said.

"You heard me." Bess shook her head in disgust. "You know you don't really deserve to be in first place . . . not after what you did today."

I totally expected Juan to avoid Bess and me. After all, that was what he had done every other time we'd tried to talk to him. But this time, he flicked the ball back to the kids and walked right over to us.

"I ride a clean race," he said, looking straight at

Bess. "You are talking about the marker—like all the reporters. How could I move it? I was *behind* Derek for most of the day!"

I had to hand it to Juan. If he was lying, he was doing a very convincing job. His broad face was filled with righteous anger.

"We saw a photograph of you giving money to some kids," I told him. "You could have paid them to move the marker for you."

"A photograph?" Juan echoed. His frown deepened. "I give money to kids all the time. And I ask for nothing in return. If you knew me, you would not question me about this marker. When I win, it's because I have ridden the best race."

Juan shoved his hands into his pockets. He began to walk away, then paused to glance back at us. "Most racers are like me. They wouldn't cheapen a race by cheating," he said over his shoulder. "You should take some advice and look to other people with your accusations."

"Other people? What do you mean?" Bess called after him.

Juan didn't answer. Keeping his back to us, he strode to the edge of the park and disappeared down the street beyond.

"Weird," I murmured, as Bess and I continued in the opposite direction. "He made it sound like he actually knows something about who moved the marker."

"Do you think he saw someone?" Bess wondered.

It was a question I couldn't begin to answer. Not without knowing more, anyway. As we walked away, I felt more dissatisfied than ever.

"Oh, brother. Things really aren't going our way tonight," Bess said, a short while later.

She and I had just stepped away from the sleek marble reception desk at the Hotel Del Rio. We'd gotten nothing but bad news from the heavyset man behind the counter.

"I can't believe we have to tell George that the massage therapists are totally booked," I said. "I guess we should have come sooner. Then we might have been able to talk to Derek. Or Paul, or even Cynthia."

We'd learned from the man at the desk that all three of them were staying at the Hotel Del Rio. It would have been the perfect opportunity to get the photograph Paul had taken and show it to Derek. Or to find out from Cynthia what she was doing for most of the day while the rest of us were freezing up on the volcanoes. Too bad for us that Derek and Cynthia were out at some meeting. And Paul wasn't around either.

"We can't exactly hang around here waiting for them. I don't want to leave George alone for too long," Bess said.

We figured that we could at least take a look at George's bike to make sure it was tuned up and ready to go. But when we checked out the courtyard where the mechanics had set up, Miguel wasn't there. He was gone on a dinner break, and the other mechanics wouldn't let anyone but George go near her bike. I tried asking them whether Miguel had ridden on the La Ruta trail that day. If he had, none of the other mechanics seemed to know about it. When we left to go back to our own hotel, we had a big fat zero to show for our trip.

Well, I guess I had a little more than nothing. Thanks to our conversation with Juan, I had even more questions swimming around inside my head. I was still mulling them over as we walked down the second-floor hallway to our room.

"I keep asking myself something," I said. "I mean, if Juan saw someone who wasn't competing in La Ruta near that marker, who could it have been?"

"Cynthia?" Bess suggested.

I frowned, sliding our key into the lock of our door and pushing it open. "I can't picture her tromping through mud and rocks to get to that marker," I said.

"Then, who?" Bess wondered.

"I'm not sure," I said. "Someone who was out there. First-aid workers, La Ruta officials, support crew, reporters. If only we could talk to Derek . . . "

George was lying on her bed in clean jeans and a T-shirt. The small television on the dresser was on, but she used the remote to switch it off as we came in. She gingerly touched her shoulder, shifting her weight against the pillows.

"Where've you guys been?" she asked.

"The Hotel Del Rio. We did our best to get you a massage, George, but they were all booked up," Bess told her. "Sorry."

George's forehead was still furrowed, and I didn't see any trace of a smile. "I don't care about that," she said. "But—"

The ringing phone on the bedside table made us all jump. George answered it, then frowned and held out the phone to Bess.

"It's for you," she mumbled.

George looked so serious that I wondered if there was bad news. But when Bess hung up a moment later, she was smiling.

"That was Paul. He's downstairs, and he's got that photograph for us," she said. "Maybe we can find Derek and show it to him."

"Derek?" George echoed. "He's all over the local news. Something about him riding off course because someone moved a marker. Is that what you were talking about before?"

I nodded. "We're trying to figure out who, so—"

103

"So you figured you'd leave your best friend totally alone?" George cut in.

She sat bolt upright, and I saw that there were tears in her eyes.

"George . . . ," I began.

"You guys just don't get it, do you!" she burst out. She jumped to her feet, then winced and rubbed her calves. "I can hardly move," she went on. "I've been sitting here wondering if I should even get on my bike tomorrow."

"We know the race has been hard for you," Bess said. She tried to touch George's arm, but George twisted away.

"You know what? I could really use my best friends right now. But all you guys can do is run all over the place worrying about how someone *else* is in danger. Thanks a lot!"

Tears streamed down her cheeks as she stormed out of our room, slamming the door behind her.

12

Disappearing Act

F or a second, Bess and I just stood there with the *bang!* of the door echoing around us. I think we were both kind of in shock. I mean, I'd never seen George so upset. Tearful outbursts just aren't her style. Which I guess should have given us a clue to how upset she was. It took a few seconds, but it finally sank in.

"We can't let her leave like that," Bess said. Grabbing her shoulder bag, she yanked the door open. "George . . . wait!" she called.

I was right behind her, but we weren't fast enough. The hallway was empty. We pounded down the stairs to the hotel lobby. Except for a guy who was standing at the reception desk, and two women who sat talking in Spanish in the sitting area inside the front door, it was empty.

"She's gone," I said, biting back my frustration. "Where do you think . . . ?"

"Bess? Nancy?" a voice spoke up behind us.

It was only then that I realized that the guy at the reception desk was Paul Maynard. I'd totally forgotten that he was waiting for us. He stood there with a manila envelope in his hand and a curious expression on his face.

"Is everything all right?" he asked. "George looked pretty upset when she left just now."

"You saw her? Where did she go? I mean, which way? Did you notice?" Bess asked, talking so fast that her words all ran together.

Paul pointed left, toward the town park. "That way, I think."

"Thanks!" Bess told him.

"Wait. Don't you want to see the photo?" Paul asked. "We were going to download all the shots in your camera, remember, Bess?"

But we were already halfway out the door. "Can't talk now, Paul. Sorry!" Bess called back to him.

We burst out onto the sidewalk, nearly ramming into a startled couple that happened to be passing by. When we got past them I saw half a dozen shops and restaurants between our hotel and the town park. We hurried along the sidewalk, peeking in at each one. At the second restaurant we checked, the kind of informal little place Paul had called a *soda*, we found her.

"George! I'm so glad we found you," I said.

George looked up from a table near the door. Her eyes were red, and tears had left moist trails on her cheeks. She was just about to take a menu from the waitress, but she stopped with her hand in midair.

"Don't you guys have something more important to do?" she asked. She took the menu from the waitress and began scanning it, without looking at us.

Okay, maybe we deserved that. But I was determined to make things right with George. And I could tell Bess was too. We slipped into the empty chairs at her table.

"Look, I don't blame you for being mad at us, George," Bess began. "I guess we didn't really get how over your head you're feeling."

"Nothing's more important to us than you," I added. "I know it might not seem that way when I've got a mystery on the brain. Sorry about that. We're so used to you being totally competent in sports. And even since La Ruta started, you keep bouncing back no matter what."

"Finishing La Ruta is really important to me," George said. "At least, it was. I really need to know you guys are behind me."

"We definitely are," I told her. "I'm sorry I let myself get distracted by all the stuff that's happened to Derek. We were so busy running around that we

107

didn't realize the best way to help you would be to just spend time with you. Can you forgive us?"

George had been fidgeting with her napkin while we spoke. When she finally looked up, I saw that her expression was softening—a little, anyway.

"You guys are my best friends," she said. "I know you didn't mean to hurt my feelings. I want to help Derek too. But . . ."

"We could be a little more sensitive to you while we're at it?" Bess guessed.

All three of us looked up as the door opened. I couldn't believe who I saw come in.

"Uh-oh . . . It's Derek and Sharine," Bess said.

The way they glanced around, I could tell they were looking for someone. It turned out to be us.

"George! I'm glad we found you," Sharine said, hurrying over. "We went to your hotel, and Paul sent us this way. I just wanted to see how you finished out today's race. You were having a tough time when I pulled ahead of you after the last checkpoint."

Derek came up next to Sharine. His tall, lanky frame seemed to fill the restaurant. "Paul said to give you this," he said, holding out a manila envelope. "Said there's a photo I should look at?"

I wasn't sure what to say. I mean, I'd been hoping to talk to Derek—and show him Paul's photo. But I didn't want to make George feel any worse than she did already.

"Um . . . this isn't a good time," I began.

"It's okay," George put in. "I know I've been acting like it's not. But Sharine and Derek and I are in La Ruta together. We could use one another's support. I don't want to be totally selfish."

"Needing your friends isn't selfish, George," Bess said.

"I want to help," George insisted. She turned and waved for the waitress. "Excuse me!" she called. "Could my friends and I move to a bigger table, please?"

George was definitely sounding more like herself. I could tell she really meant what she said. Soon the five of us were sitting at a new table sipping sodas while we waited for our grilled steak, marinated fish, and a salad made of hearts of palm with lime juice.

"Hmm," Derek said, when we showed him the photograph Paul had taken of Juan and the kids along the race route on Irazú. "We passed through so many villages. . . . And I was ahead of Juan, so I didn't see him stop. You really think he paid those kids to move the marker?"

"Maybe. Not that we have any concrete proof," I said. "Juan hinted at something else—that maybe someone who's *not* competing in La Ruta moved the marker."

"Someone else?" Sharine spoke up. "But, who?"

I still wasn't sure it made sense to tell Derek about our suspicions of Cynthia. But with just one day left in the race, how could we not? Taking a deep breath, I told him and Sharine about the conversation Bess and I had overheard the day before.

"Cynthia doesn't really want me to get hurt," Derek said right away. "Sure, she's dramatic. But it's just a way to play up the attacks so Aqua Trim will make a better deal."

"We just met with her. She said she was teleconferencing with their people for most of the day," Sharine added. "That's why she wasn't at any of the checkpoints."

"She'd never actually put me in danger," Derek insisted. "I'm sure of it."

I wish I felt as confident as he did. But when we all went back to our hotels after eating, Cynthia and Juan were both still on my list of suspects.

"Wow. George is really doing great," I said, the next morning.

Our Jeep was climbing a rocky road alongside George, Sharine, and a bunch of other riders who were at the center of the pack. The road looked like it was made of boulders, and our teeth chattered nonstop as the Jeep thumped over them. Still, the bumpy ride hadn't slowed George down. She seemed really pumped up and determined, moving up in the pack and pedaling faster than I would have thought possible.

The weather was as hot and steamy as it had been during Stage One. We were heading through jungle and had seen tons of white-faced capuchin monkeys, sloths, and parrots. Every time we passed through a village—with six or seven houses and maybe a tiny *soda*—kids waved and cheered. Bess grinned as she snapped a photograph of a little girl reaching up to slap George's hand in a high five.

"If she keeps up this pace, she'll finish the race way before the cutoff time," Bess said. "I'm not doing so bad myself, either—at taking pictures, I mean. We should have some great shots to show our families when we get back home."

Bess was still snapping photos when George rode up alongside us a few minutes later. "Sharine and I were just talking," she said breathlessly. "We're fine, and we've got each other. Maybe you two should drive ahead and see how Derek's doing."

"I'm not sure that's a great idea," Bess said, shooting a sideways glance at me. "What if you crash again . . . or your shoulder starts hurting? You might need us."

"My shoulder's much better. No bleeding or anything," George said. "I never thought I'd say this, but I think Derek's the one who needs you today.

I mean, it's the last day of the race. If someone is going to hurt him, today is the day."

That thought had definitely crossed my mind. But I still found myself hesitating.

"Please," Sharine said, riding up next to George. "George and I promised that we'd stay near each other today no matter what. We want to finish La Ruta together. I wish you guys would check on Derek."

George and Sharine were right. Derek could be in danger, so Bess and I gave in. Picking up our pace, we steered the Jeep around the ATV in front of us.

Dozens of racers had dropped out of La Ruta since day one. Still, it wasn't easy to get past all the bikers and support crews that were still on the road. It took us about fifteen minutes to reach the front riders. We finally caught sight of Derek, riding on a muddy downhill section.

"He's all right!" Bess said, peering through the lens of Paul's camera. "And he's ahead of Juan."

But no sooner did I spot them than the race course veered off the main road. A narrow, single track disappeared into a thick mass of palms, jacaranda trees, ferns, and vines. There was no way we could follow in our Jeep.

"Wait a sec. Paul showed me how to use the zoom lens," Bess murmured. She pressed a button, and the lens moved smoothly outward. "Yes—I can still see them. It looks like they're heading onto some kind of bridge."

"Bridge? What kind of bridge?" I asked. Pulling over to the side, I grabbed my binoculars and adjusted them. Yup, the path led to a bridge, all right—a rickety-looking thing made of rope and wooden slats suspended over a wide, muddy river.

"Oh, my gosh!" Bess gasped as Derek's bike skidded on the slats. "Maybe he should get off and walk. It looks slippery!"

That was for sure. As we watched, Derek's tires skidded a second time. "Oh, no!" I cried.

The wheels of Derek's bike slipped to the side and he fell. Through the binoculars, I saw the whole bridge shudder. Derek and his bike slid toward the edge of the bridge. Except for a few ropes, there was nothing to stop him from falling off.

"Hang on, Derek," I murmured. "Hang on!"

Scrambling, Derek caught a rope in the crook of his elbow. His legs dangled off the side of the bridge, but he managed to hold on to his bike with his other hand.

"Uh-oh. Nancy—look who's coming up behind him," Bess said.

I swung my binoculars to see Juan ride his mountain bike onto the bridge. The bridge started to sway even more. Derek struggled to hang on to the rope. But what worried me the most was the look of incredible determination on Juan's face as he rode toward Derek.

13

Close Call

D erek!" Bess shouted. "Look out behind you!"

Not that Derek could hear us. I flung open the door of the Jeep and jumped out onto road. "We can't just sit here," I said. "We've got to help him!"

But the muddy rocks were so slippery that I kept stumbling. Even without my binoculars, I could see Juan bearing down on Derek. It was like watching a horror movie. . . . My stomach was churning. I wanted to help, but I was powerless.

"Nancy . . . he's stopping!" Bess breathed.

I lifted my binoculars in time to see Juan, still straddling his bike, reach toward Derek. Derek's face was filled with fear as Juan bent over him. My muscles were so tight that I couldn't move or breathe.

In the next instant, Juan's hands closed around Derek's forearm. I had to blink a few times before I realized what was happening.

"He's *helping* Derek," I said, letting out the breath I'd been holding.

It still made me nervous to see how unsteadily the bridge swayed. Juan gave Derek a hand up and helped him to get his bike upright again. Both of them walked their bikes the rest of the way across the bridge. Seconds later, they disappeared on the trail behind the thick trunks of some overarching trees.

"That was close," Bess said when she lowered her camera at last.

My heart was still pounding as we got back into the Jeep. "Maybe we were wrong about Juan," I said, thinking out loud. "It doesn't make sense that he would help Derek if he's the one who's been sabotaging him."

"Then who could it be?" Bess asked.

I drove forward on the bumpy road as fast as I dared. "Maybe Juan can help us figure that out. Let's try to talk to him at the next checkpoint."

"There they are!" Bess said, about an hour later.

We had only just gotten to the checkpoint—at the foot of a muddy downhill trail. The road we had taken had crossed through small farms, meandering cow paths, and a couple of different rivers. I was finally getting used to seeing toucans and parrots, and having monkeys scold us from the trees. Bess even got some pictures of crocodiles sunning themselves on the banks of one of the rivers we crossed. But the truth was, I was too preoccupied to really appreciate the scenery. I was relieved to see Derek come skidding to a stop at the checkpoint, just a dozen feet behind Juan.

They both zeroed in on the La Ruta truck, grabbing sandwiches and drinks. Cameras clicked as news crews moved in around them.

"Looks like this one's going to be a nail-biter," I heard Paul Maynard call out. "Any predictions on who's going to win?"

Derek just held up a hand. "I'll leave the predictions to you," he said, after gulping down half a bottle of water. "My job is just to ride the best race I can."

"Any attacks so far today?" another reporter called out.

Derek just pushed past the reporters, shaking his head. "No more questions," he said. "I'm fine. Everything is fine."

He looked relieved when Cynthia strode into the circle of reporters. "The race is still on," she reminded them. "I can take questions for Derek. . . . "

Now that Derek was moving away from the press, Bess and I went over to him.

"We saw what happened on the bridge," I told him.

Derek was spraying water from his squeeze bottle onto his face. "I know what you're thinking, but it wasn't sabotage. I just slipped," he said, as water dripped down his jersey. "If Juan hadn't helped me out . . . "

He didn't finish, but I knew what he meant. Derek might have lost a lot more than the race. "Why *did* you help, Juan?" I asked, turning to look at him.

Juan was readjusting his helmet a few feet away. He shrugged, glancing at us as he straddled his bike. "I want to win La Ruta, yes," he said. "But I would never ride past someone who is in danger." With that, he pushed off down the race course. "I'll be waiting for you at the finish," he called to Derek over his shoulder.

"Not if I get there first," Derek muttered. Grunting, he took off after Juan.

I couldn't help wishing they'd stuck around for just a few more seconds. There was so much more I wanted to ask them. "I keep thinking about what Juan said yesterday, when we saw him in the Turrialba town park," I said.

"Hmmm?" Bess murmured. She snapped some photographs of Derek and Juan, then turned her camera toward the crowd near the La Ruta truck.

"We need to think about other suspects," I said. "He could have pushed Derek right off that bridge, but—"

"What did you say?" a sharp voice cut in.

I turned to see Cynthia standing next to us with her hands planted on her hips. "Someone tried to push Derek off a bridge? Why didn't you tell me?"

The way her eyes were gleaming, I could tell she was already thinking of how to turn the story into a major headline in sports news.

"Actually, he wasn't pushed," Bess said. "He slipped, and almost fell off. Juan Santiago helped him across."

"Helped him?" Cynthia's smile faltered. "You're sure?"

I nodded. "Derek said so himself. There wasn't any attack this time," I told her.

She didn't exactly look thrilled to hear that. But apparently Cynthia wasn't about to let the truth stop her from getting good publicity for Derek. After Bess and I told her what had happened, she practically raced back to the reporters. I heard her say something about "suspiciously slick boards" on the suspension bridge and how Derek had "overcome incredible odds to stay neck and neck with Juan Santiago."

Bess and I didn't bother to stick around for the whole story. As we walked away, Bess aimed the camera at a group of locals who had gathered to watch. She pressed the shutter, then frowned when nothing happened.

"The memory card is full," she said, peering at the camera's tiny screen. "I'll have to download these photos before I can take more."

"Well, Paul offered to help you download them yesterday. Maybe he can show you now," I said.

More riders had started to arrive at the checkpoint. I could barely make out Paul's ponytail and red Hawaiian shirt. He and the other journalists thronged both sides of the trail. So did the support crews and the usual crowd of onlookers. There were so many people that I held back while Bess made her way over to Paul. She came back a minute later holding up a car key.

"Voila!" she said, grinning. "Paul told me what to do. The computer's with all his other stuff in the backseat. He'll e-mail the pictures to us later, so I can pull them up on my computer at home. We just have to lock up and give him the key when we're done."

Paul's car hadn't gotten any neater since the last time we'd been in it. His computer and camera cases lay in a messy jumble on the backseat, alongside some empty water bottles and a crumpled Hawaiian shirt. Instead of trying to make room for ourselves, we took the computer from its case and opened it on the hood of the car. Bess went to work, and before long, a series of thumbnail photographs appeared on the screen. She clicked on the first one with the mouse, and it appeared at full size on the screen.

"Remember that?" Bess said, smiling at the digital image of George in the middle of the pack at Punta Leona.

One by one, Bess clicked on the thumbnail shots. It was like a virtual tour of the last few days. Seeing some of the photos of George—with rain beating down on her and blood staining her jersey—made me realize all over again how hard La Ruta had been for her. And when I saw a shot of Derek, scraped up and scowling after his brakes were cut, I found myself hoping he was okay right now—wherever he was.

"Ooops! I must have clicked on the wrong icon," Bess said, breaking into my thoughts. "Where'd my photos go?"

The thumbnail photographs had disappeared from the screen, I realized. Instead, about half a dozen folders were displayed.

"Which one are my photos in?" Bess wondered. With a shrug, she moved the arrow to one of the folders and clicked on it. A grid of tiny images flashed onto the screen, but when Bess clicked on the first one, it wasn't the photograph of George.

"Hey—that's Derek," I said, peering at the image of him punching a fist victoriously into the air at the end of a race. But as I looked closer, I saw that Derek was in a city, not the rain forest, and the street signs in the background were in English. "These photos aren't even of Costa Rica. It must be a race he was in someplace else," I said.

Bess frowned at the screen. "I guess my photos are in a different folder, huh?" she said. She was about to clear the screen, but as she reached for the mouse pad, I noticed the caption beneath the photograph.

"Oh, my gosh . . . Bess, look!" I pointed at the words that had been typed beneath the photograph: *Smug idiot wins again.*

"'Smug idiot . . . ,'" Bess said, reading the caption. "That's not exactly a compliment. . . . "

She was already clicking on the next thumbnail shot. It, too, was of Derek, but his hair was longer and he looked a little younger. The caption read: *I can get to you.*

Just looking at the words made the hairs stand up on the back on my neck. "Sound familiar?" I said.

"You mean, like the threatening notes Derek got?" Bess said. "I can't believe what I'm thinking, Nancy."

"That maybe Paul hates Derek enough to slip him threatening notes and sabotage his bike?" I said.

Bess's face had definitely gotten paler. "But . . . he's been so nice to us," she said. "I mean, can the guy who's been flirting with me be the same one who did all those awful things to Derek? It doesn't make sense!"

It *was* kind of hard to believe. "Let's look at some more shots," I said.

Bess clicked on the next image, and the next, on and on. They were all of Derek. Not every photograph had a caption, but the ones that did were so threatening and angry that it made me squirm to read them.

"I don't get it," Bess said, when we exited from the screen. "I mean, *why* does Paul hate Derek so much?"

I glanced toward the crowd at the checkpoint, but it was so mobbed I didn't see Paul. "Keep an eye out for him. I'm going to look around. Maybe we'll find something that will help us understand."

I yanked open the car door and rummaged around in the backseat. I wasn't sure what I was looking for—a note, or some clue that Paul had cut Derek's brakes, or . . . *anything* that would link him to the notes or the attacks. Too bad there was nothing among the empty bottles and camera cases. Leaning forward, I rifled through some papers in the front of the car.

"Race pamphlets, maps . . . Hey, wait a minute!" I murmured.

I had just popped open the glove compartment. Lying there, on top of the manual, was a black nylon tool kit. I grabbed it and opened it—and then let out a whistle.

"Sharine told me the tools in Derek's kit had yellow handles," I told Bess. "Look at this." I held up a socket wrench that had a bright yellow rubber handle. "Plus, some of the tools are missing."

"Which makes sense, since whoever took Derek's kit dropped a couple wrenches in the hotel lobby back in Punta Leone," Bess said. "So Paul *is* the one who's been sabotaging Derek." She bit her lip, staring out the mud-splattered window. "Wow."

I still didn't understand why, but I didn't think we could afford to wait around trying to figure it out. "The good news is that Paul is here, and not anywhere near Derek," I said. I climbed out of the car, shaded my eyes from the sun, and peered at the crowd at the checkpoint. "Do you see Paul?"

Bess shook her head. I tried to ignore the nagging worries that popped up in my mind, but I couldn't. "We'd better take a look around," I said.

I put Paul's computer back in its case and locked it inside his car. After putting his car key and Derek's tool kit in my bag, Bess and I headed toward the checkpoint. For the next five minutes, we searched through the crowd next to the trail, the first-aid tent, and even the inside of the truck where La Ruta officials were handing out sandwiches and drinks.

"He isn't anywhere," Bess said, shooting me a worried glance.

"Oh, he's somewhere," I said grimly. "And I'd bet anything that he's causing trouble for Derek."

14

Chase Through the Jungle

A dark feeling settled over me as I stared ahead down the race route. The road had dipped to a low at the checkpoint. Beyond, it rose again, and scrubby farmland gave way to more forest.

"How are we going to find him?" Bess wondered.

"He can't have gone very far," I said, thinking it out. "I mean, he didn't even take his car. And it doesn't make sense that he'd go on foot. He'd never catch up to Derek."

My eyes jumped all over as I spoke—to the crowd and the line of support vehicles lining the sides of the road, to the trees of the rain forest ahead. . . . I guess I was looking for some clue to where Paul might be—and what he might be up to.

"Hey, isn't that Carlos?" Bess said.

She was pointing at the La Ruta service truck. Sure enough, one of the people standing next to the truck was the guy with spiked hair who had driven Paul's car the day before while Paul took photos on the race route.

Bess and I reached him in about five seconds flat. "Carlos! Have you seen Paul? Paul Maynard, the photographer. You drove his car for him yesterday?" Bess asked breathlessly.

Carlos stared at us blankly. I guess he was having a hard time understanding our English. Luckily, one of the guys in the La Ruta truck translated for us. *"Ah, si!"* Carlos said, nodding. He said something else in Spanish, gesturing toward the first-aid tent.

"He says your friend Paul borrowed a bicycle from one of the riders who had to drop out," the guy in the truck told us. "He took off about ten minutes ago."

"Which means he's hot on Derek's trail," I said. "Come on. We've got to catch up to him!"

My heart pounded as we ran to our Jeep and started down the road. Now that the top riders had passed through, more and more bikers and support vehicles were filling the road. Even though Paul only had a ten-minute lead on us, we couldn't seem to get ahead of the pack.

"Whoa . . . ," Bess said, as the road crested a hill and there was break in the trees.

Ahead of us, the road descended toward a coastal plain—a flat jungle that stretched to the east as far as we could see. After all the hills and mountains we had crossed, it was an amazing sight.

"We must be getting closer to the Atlantic coast," Bess said.

"Too bad the traffic is so heavy. It's worse than ever," I said, frowning at the mob of bikers, cars, and trucks. From where we were, they looked like a swarm of ants moving down toward the flat jungle below. I kept looking for Paul's red Hawaiian shirt, but I hadn't seen it yet.

"According to the literature, the race route moves off this road and follows some old railway track," Bess said. "Trains used to transport bananas from the coastal plantations, but the tracks were abandoned when trucks took over about twenty-five years ago."

I really worried when I heard that. "We won't be able to drive on a train track," I said. "We'll have to catch up to Paul *before* the turn off."

I did everything I could to pass other ATVs, but the cyclists seemed to be moving faster than the support vehicles. By the time the road flattened out, as we hit the coastal plain, I still hadn't spotted Paul.

"I can't believe this!" I said, banging my hands against the steering wheel in frustration. "What if we . . ."

At that moment, I caught sight of a bike tire sticking out from the scruffy palm fronds that grew alongside the road. "Hold on," I said, slowing down. "There's a bike. Wait—make that *two* bikes!"

The bikes looked as if they had been abandoned. No one was near them, and their tires lay twisted at an angle to the frame, as if they'd been hurriedly tossed aside. One of them, I didn't recognize. But the other one . . .

"It's Derek's!" Bess breathed. She pointed at the number 139 that dangled from the handlebars. "Do you think Paul caught up with him?" she asked, frowning at the other bicycle.

"Looks like it," I said. I gazed into the jungle. Was it my imagination, or were there some crushed ferns and moss where someone had walked? "Come on. We'd better see if we can find them."

We got out on foot and tried to find a trail. If we saw a crushed plant, or an indentation in the mossy ground, we followed it. Everything around us looked emerald green—the palms, the mossy trunks of high-arching trees, the vines that climbed up to the leafy canopy above. The air was so humid that Bess and I were both sweating.

"See anything?" Bess whispered.

"Not yet," I said. We were making our way around

a thick stand of saplings. A bright blue butterfly fluttered among the slender trunks. Monkeys and birds chirped and chattered in the branches above. I thought I heard the sound of rushing water, and as we rounded the trees, I caught sight of a river beyond.

We had already taken a few steps toward it when I saw a flash of red moving along the riverbank. This was no scarlet macaw or wild orchid, that was for sure. It was Paul Maynard, pushing Derek along the riverbank in front of him. Derek's arms were tied behind his back. As he stumbled along the bank in front of Paul, he kept shooting terrified glances down at the water.

I grabbed Bess's arm and we both stopped short. I saw the scared glimmer in Bess's eyes as she took in the scene.

"Nancy . . . look!" she whispered. "On the river-bank."

I had been so busy staring at Paul and Derek that I hadn't noticed anything special about the river. Now I saw that it rushed over a rocky bed about ten feet below the top of the bank. Sunlight filtering through the trees sparkled on the water, but that wasn't what Bess had noticed.

What she had noticed were the six giant-size crocodiles that sat sunning themselves at the water's edge, just below Derek and Paul.

15

On the Edge

Paul's going to push him off!" Bess squeaked out.

As Paul shoved Derek closer to the edge, his cycling shoes kicked dirt down the embankment. The shower of pebbles and earth seemed to rouse the crocodiles. I shivered as two of them lifted themselves up onto their squat legs and pointed their long snouts up the embankment.

"Stop!" I yelled.

I ran toward them. Paul swung his head to look in our direction. He didn't exactly look happy to see us. Far from it.

"Stop right there, or you can say good-bye to Derek!" he growled. He shoved a hand into Derek's back, making him teeter precariously at the edge of the bank.

"D-do what he says!" Derek said, scrambling to keep from falling.

Bess and I both stopped short, about twenty feet away from them. "Take it easy," I said, holding up my hands. "Don't do anything crazy."

"We know you're the one who's been sabotaging Derek," Bess added. "We found his tool kit in your glove compartment."

Paul nodded when he saw the tool kit I pulled from my bag. "Congratulations," he said. "Not that it will do Derek any good."

I didn't like the sound of that—or the way Paul kept pushing and pulling on the ropes that bound Derek's wrists. Each time he gave a little push, the movement startled the crocodiles. They weren't climbing the riverbank—not yet, anyway. But Derek turned a little whiter every time one of them stirred.

"Why'd you do it?" I asked, gulping back my own fear. "You've been so nice to Bess and me. What did Derek do to deserve this?"

I thought I saw a glimmer of regret in his eyes. But his look hardened as he turned toward Derek. "You don't have any clue, do you?" he said. Not that he gave Derek a chance to answer. "Of course not. You were too busy collecting prize money to remember that *you're* the one who caused the crash that ended my racing career."

Derek whipped his head around to gape at Paul. "What!" he exclaimed. "I wasn't anywhere near you. I had already pulled ahead when you got caught in that pileup."

"An accident *you* caused by cutting in front of the pack on the downhill," Paul said angrily.

I looked back and forth between the two guys. "Look, Derek obviously didn't mean to cause any harm," I began.

"Besides, now you're a fantastic photographer, Paul," Bess added. "Maybe that accident helped you to find something you're even better at than mountain-biking."

Paul didn't seem to have heard her. Scowling at Derek, he said, "I would have won that race if it hadn't been for you. *I'm* the one who should have been riding at the head of the pack for the past three years, not you!"

He spat the words out, his face red with fury.

"T-take it easy!" Derek sputtered.

Paul was so angry that he wasn't even looking at Bess and me anymore. Slowly, I began moving toward him.

Hmm, I thought, as I spotted a coconut lying among the ferns beneath a palm tree. Moving quickly, I scooped it up and held it behind my back.

"I, uh . . . sorry, Paul," Derek mumbled. He shot a quick glance our way, and understanding flashed in his eyes. "I didn't realize how you felt."

Paul shook his head in disgust. "That figures. To you, I'm just the guy who makes you look good in magazines," he scoffed. "You never knew that every time you won a race, I hated you more."

"Is that why you sent me those threatening notes?" Derek asked. He gulped, eyeing the crocodiles below.

Don't give up, I begged silently. Bess and I took another step, and another. *If you can just keep distracting Paul a little longer . . . .*

"I couldn't take watching you win any more," Paul muttered. "I had to do something. But even threats didn't stop you from winning."

"So you decided to sabotage me to make sure I didn't win La Ruta," Derek guessed.

"That's right," Paul told him. "It was easy getting your tool kit. I just had the desk page you. But I needed a little help to slice your brakes and move that marker. Luckily, little children are very gullible."

Derek scowled over his shoulder at Paul. "You let us think it was Juan who paid the kids, but all along it was you."

"It was worth it," Paul said smugly. "La Ruta is one race the great Derek McDaniel *isn't* going to win. . . . "

Bess and I were just half a dozen feet away from them now. Slowly, I raised the coconut into throwing position.

Paul whirled around to face Bess and me, but it was too late. The coconut was already flying through the air. It hit the side of his head with a *thunk* that made me wince. Half a second later, Paul slumped to the ground, unconscious.

"Boy, am I glad to see you!" Derek breathed.

I shivered as I caught a glimpse of the crocodiles' beady eyes staring at us from the river's edge.

"Help me with this rope, Bess," I said, yanking Derek away from the embankment. "We need to get out of here and call the police, before Paul comes to. When George crosses the finish line, we have to be there!"

"There she is!" Bess cried, a few hours later.

She and I were standing at the finish line for La Ruta de los Conquistadores. Once again, we were at the ocean, only this time it was the Atlantic Ocean. Barriers had been set up along the beach where the race ended. A huge crowd pressed against them, clapping and shouting while the wide fronds of palm and banana trees swayed in the breeze.

Bikers had been arriving in clusters ever since Bess and I got to the beach after handing Paul over to the local police. I spotted George and Sharine at the front of the cluster that was now arriving. They both looked tired, and their cycling jerseys were soaked with sweat.

"Go, George! Go, Sharine!" I yelled. With so many

people cheering, I wasn't sure they would hear me. But then George looked right at Bess and me, and a grin lit up her face. She and Sharine both whooped as they crossed the finish line. Instead of slowing down, they rode farther onto the beach, until the soft sand stopped them. Jumping off their bikes, they ran to the water, yanking off their helmets and tossing them aside before diving into the surf in their clothes. When they came out, dripping with seawater, they dropped breathlessly onto the hard-packed sand just beyond where the waves broke.

"You did it!" Bess exclaimed. "And the cutoff isn't for another hour!"

George grinned up at us as we crouched next to her. "I really did," she agreed. "Crocodiles, bumpy railroad tracks, rickety bridges, and all."

"How's Derek?" Sharine asked. She propped herself up with one arm and looked worriedly around.

"Fine . . . now. He can tell you himself, if reporters ever give him a break," I said.

I nodded toward a tented canopy that had been set up on the beach. Dozens of racers milled around near the buffet tables beneath the tent. Derek and Cynthia stood just outside, surrounded by TV cameras and reporters. But when Derek caught sight of Sharine and George, he broke away and hurried toward us.

"Look at all those reporters," Sharine said, as he

gave her a hug. "Did you win? You must have, to be getting so much attention from the press."

"Well, not exactly," Derek said. "I took an unexpected detour, thanks to Paul Maynard. . . . "

Sharine and George sat there in the sand, looking more and more surprised, as Derek, Bess, and I told them the whole story.

"Wow! So it was Paul all along," George said when we were done. "Someone who wasn't competing in La Ruta, just like Juan told you."

"We asked him about that when we got here," Bess said. "It turns out that Juan saw Paul giving money to some kids—back in Punta Leona and again along the race route on Irazú."

"It's a good thing Nancy and Bess found me when they did," Derek said. "I didn't win La Ruta, but at least I didn't end up being lunch for a bunch of crocodiles."

"Thank goodness," George said, shivering. "And we all made it to the finish line before the cutoff."

"All I care about right now is making it to the buffet table," Sharine said. "I'm starved!"

She and George were soaking wet and covered with sand. But they looked totally happy as we headed over to the tented area where the food was. As we passed the reporters, Cynthia stepped away from them and came over to us.

"Derek! I've got great news," she told him, barely

glancing at the rest of us. "I just closed the deal with Aqua Trim, for almost twice what they originally offered."

"Let me guess," Bess put in. "Once you told them all about what Paul Maynard did, they wanted to be first to cash in on Derek's new publicity?"

"Isn't it marvelous?" Cynthia practically squealed.

"Oh, yeah. I'm sure getting threatened and nearly killed a few times was *really* marvelous for Derek," George said dryly.

Still, I noticed that the smile stayed on her face when some race officials came up to her at the buffet table and congratulated her on her finish.

"I hope we'll see you both at La Ruta again next year," the official said, shaking hands with George, and then Sharine.

I thought George would choke on the slice of mango she had just popped into her mouth. Instead, she chewed thoughtfully and swallowed before answering.

"You never know," she said at last. Then she grinned at Bess and me—a wide smile that was warmer than the tropical sun just setting to the west. "Anything is possible. But next time I come to Costa Rica, I might try something more relaxing—like white-water rafting down a river packed with crocodiles."

"Bite your tongue! You don't mean that," Bess chided.

I was pretty sure George was joking too. But when it comes to her and sports, you can never be *totally* sure.

REDISCOVER THE CLASSIC MYSTERIES OF NANCY DREW

$5.99 ($8.99 CAN) each
AVAILABLE AT YOUR LOCAL BOOKSTORE OR LIBRARY

Grosset & Dunlap • A division of Penguin Young Readers Group
A member of Penguin Group (USA), Inc. • A Pearson Company
www.penguin.com/youngreaders